ARCHITECTURE
SHOWN TO THE CHILDREN

This edition published 2025
by Living Book Press
Copyright © Living Book Press, 2025

ISBN: 978-1-76153-853-7 (hardcover)
          978-1-76153-824-7 (softcover)

First published in 1913.

A catalogue record for this book is available from the National Library of Australia

ARCHITECTURE SHOWN TO THE CHILDREN

by

GLADYS WYNNE

AMIENS CATHEDRAL
(SEE PP. 82, 93, 123)

Contents

INTRODUCTORY

ARCHITECTURE means beautiful or artistic building. Everyone builds in a fashion. Bees build, beavers build, birds build, men build. Our forefathers did not need much architecture when they lived in caves and dens of the earth; and even when they came to the surface, a tent, or wooden hut, or straw roof supported on poles formed sufficient shelter for them. It was not till thousands of years later that they began to build in stone.

Their first houses would be of the simplest description — just four walls and a roof to keep out the rain, and windows and a door to let them out and in (Fig. 1). But by and by, the love of beauty, which is an instinct in human nature, would assert itself, and they would want to adorn their house.

They might put a little cap above the windows or pillars beside the door; or they might work mouldings between the door and windows or carry the outlines of the roof into gables and turrets, and domes and spires. Till at last, instead

FIG. 1. - CROFTER'S COTTAGE

of a bare up-and-down flat wall, they would have a beautiful building, full of character and interest.

Figure 2 is a perfectly plain window.

Figure 3 has mouldings. If you compare the two, you will see what a difference the mouldings make.

Great architecture is seen best in the temples of the gods, as we should expect. The builders strove with each other which of them should make these the most beautiful, and the one who succeeded best got the name of "ARCHITECT," which means "MASTER BUILDER." We have many builders now, but few master builders. It is of the master builders and their work that we speak when we use the words Architect and Architecture.

GREEK AND GOTHIC

The first thing that strikes one in studying buildings is the variety of styles. Here is one all turrets and gables and round towers, with staircases inside, and all sorts of odd nooks and

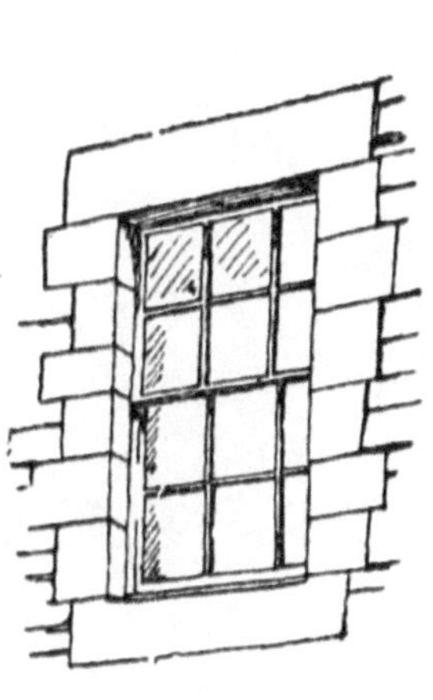

FIG. 2. - PLAIN WINDOW

FIG. 3. - WINDOW WITH MOULDINGS

corners that you would like to explore; and then, again, you come upon another that is square and regular and "coldly fair." The one is Gothic, the other Greek.

These are the two principal styles, and when you know these two, you know a good deal; because the others are more or less related to them — descendants, or second or third cousins, so to speak, twice removed, and with a different name, of course.

There are much older styles than the Greek. There are the Egyptian, the Indian, and the Assyrian; but we cannot study everything, and it is best to begin with the styles nearer home, which we can see examples of in our own country or in Europe. These are:— the Greek, Roman, Byzantine, Romanesque or Norman, and the Gothic. The Renaissance, which followed the Gothic, is a revival of the Greek and Roman.

CHAPTER I

GREEK ARCHITECTURE

THE DORIC COLUMN (FIG. 5)

THIS chapter is about columns. "A column" is the grand word for a pillar. Let us look at one — a real good look, not the passing glance we generally bestow. Columns are like people; they are so much more interesting when you really know them.

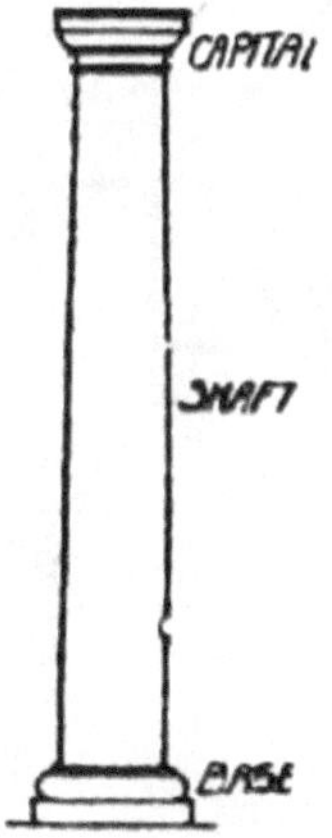

A column (Fig. 4) consists of three parts:

A base to stand on,

A long body called the shaft, and

A head or capital.

Of these, the base is the least important. It may even be wanting, but we cannot have a column without a shaft or capital, any more than we can have a person without a body or head.

There are many kinds of columns. The

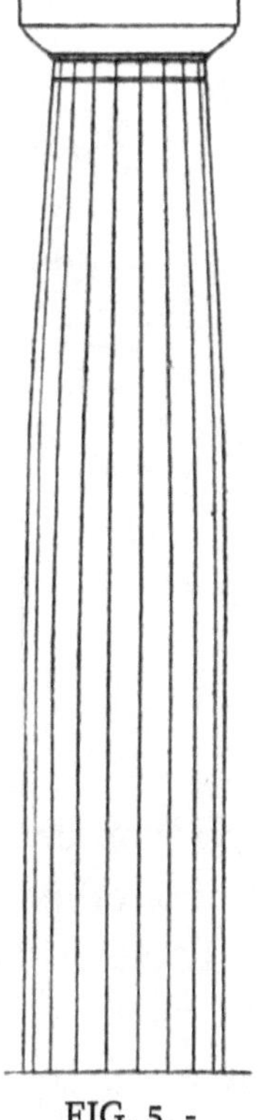

FIG. 4. - GREEK

FIG. 5. -
PARTHENON
COLUMN.

1

three we are going to look at are among the commonest; you will meet them everywhere. But they do not belong to this country. They are strangers in a strange land and have traveled all the way from sunny Greece.

The best-known and the plainest of the three is the Doric (Fig. 5). It is short and sturdy, with a simple capital and no base. To look at it, you would think the Doric column was quite straight, but it grows the least bit narrower towards the top, like the trunk of a tree, and it has a slight swelling about the middle. The narrow grooves or channels all around the column are called "flutings." You will get the idea of a flut-

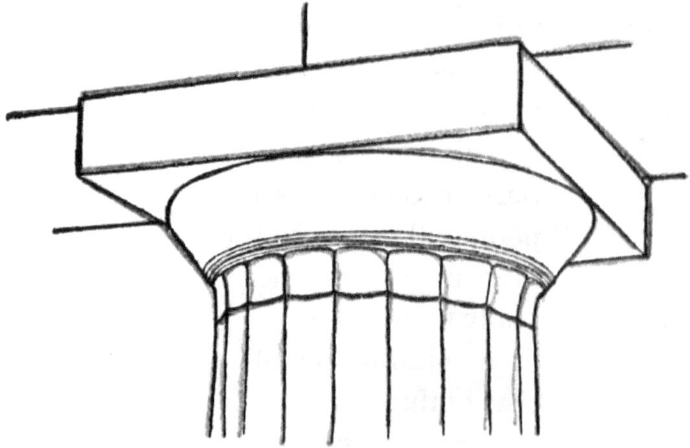

FIG. 6. - DORIC CAPITAL

ing if you divide a reed pipe into two its whole length and then put the two halves back to back with their edges.

The Doric capital is very simple (Fig. 6). It consists of two parts, a sloping one below called the "echinus" and a square slab above, which rests on the lower part like the hat on the top of a head. This is the "abacus," which means a board or tile.

THE IONIC COLUMN (Fig. 7)

The Ionic column is a contrast to the Doric. It is slender and graceful and has a base, a capital, and flutings, which are deeper than the Doric and more numerous. But the capital is its distinguishing feature. It reminds one of rams' horns or, as some people think, of a young lady's curls, the horns or curls being known as "volutes" (Fig. 8). One peculiarity of the Ionic capital has been a good deal criticized: namely, the front and the sides are not alike, the profile differing from the full face as much as it does in most humans.

Every column has its favourite moulding, just as every young lady has her favourite ornament, and the favourite moulding of the Ionic is the "egg-and-dart," so called from its supposed resemblance to an egg and an arrow (Fig. 9). Some people think that this moulding had an allegorical meaning, the "egg" typifying "Life," which usually originates in an egg, and the "arrow" "Death."

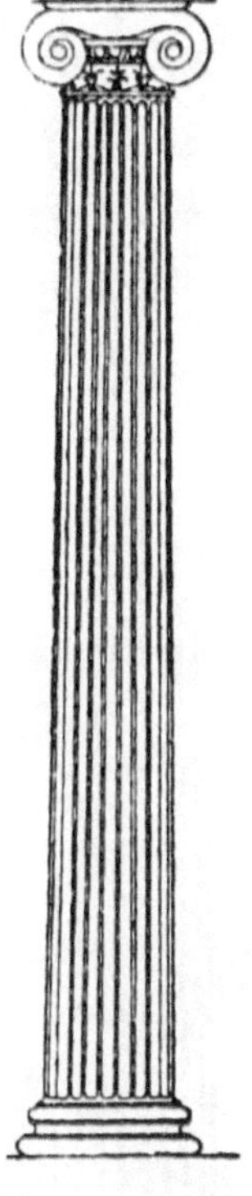

FIG. 7. – GREEK IONIC COLUMN

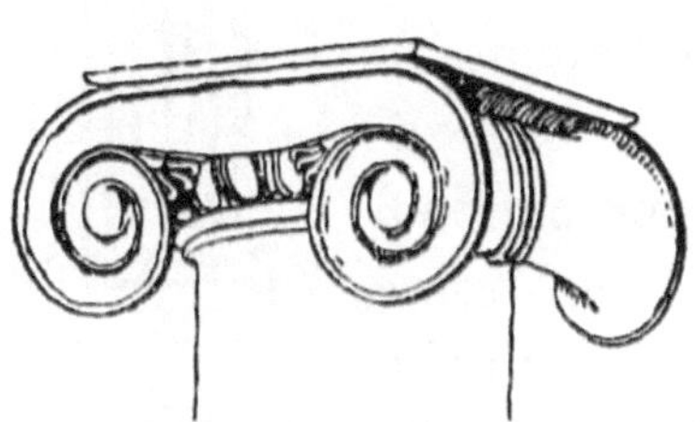

FIG. 8. - GREEK IONIC CAPITAL

FIG. 9. - GREEK EGG AND DART

THE CORINTHIAN COLUMN (FIG. 10)

The Corinthian is the third and last member of our little Greek family. It is the most ornamental of the three, and the greatest favourite, with the Romans at least, who admired it so much that they adopted it. This column has a base and flutings like the Ionic, but its capital is quite different. It consists of two parts, a leafy one below and a square flat slab above (Fig. 11). There is a pretty story told about the origin of this capital. It is said that a young girl in Corinth, having died, her nurse collected all her little toys and ornaments in a basket and put them on the grave, covering them with a tile to keep them from being blown away. This basket was placed on the root of an Acanthus, the Greek thistle (Fig. 12), which, though pressed down by the weight, shot up its stem and leaves in the spring, taking graceful curves and bends at the angles of the tile. Now, it so happened that when it was looking its best, a famous sculptor passed by, and, stopping to admire, suddenly the thought came to him that this basket, with its delicate foliage, would make a beautiful and original capital for a column. So he hastened home and experimented, and the graceful Corinthian capital which you see here was the result.

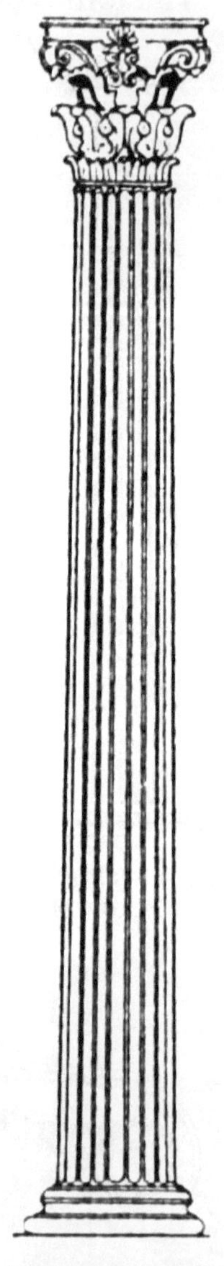

FIG. 10. - GREEK CORINTHIAN COLUMN.

FIG. 11. - GREEK
CORINTHIAN CAPITAL

FIG. 12. - ACANTHUS

THE ENTABLATURE

Such, then, were the three Greek columns, and, according as a temple was built with the one or the other, it was said to belong to the Doric, the Ionic, or the Corinthian ORDER.

But there is more to be considered in the Greek "Order" than the columns. There is the ENTABLATURE.

This is a long word. Let us try to guess the meaning. You will see that the second syllable almost spells TABLE—EN-TABL-ature; and the entablature has just this likeness to a table, that both are flat. It is the flat block or beam that rests on the columns and supports the roof (Fig. 13).

Like the columns, the entablature consists of three parts:—

1. The Cornice.
2. The Frieze.
3. The Architrave.

Cornice means "Crown." It is at the top and crowns the whole entablature. The Frieze is the middle, and the Architrave is below all. Architrave means "Chief Beam." It rests immediately on the columns; that is why it is called Archi- trave. The Archbishop is the chief bishop, and the Archi- trave is the chief beam.

FIG. 13. - GREEK DORIC ENTABLATURE

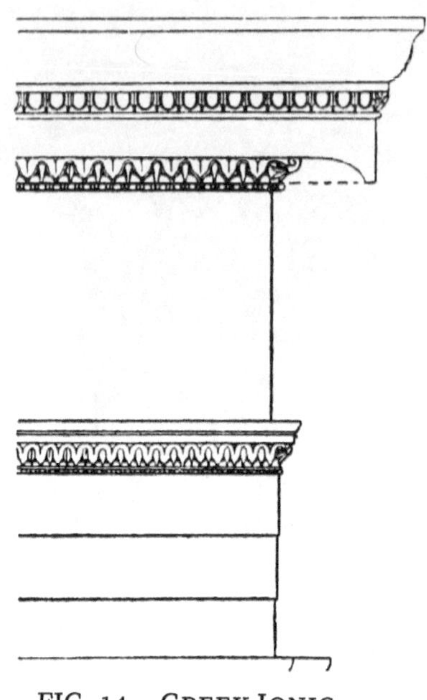

FIG. 14. - GREEK IONIC ENTABLATURE (ERECHTHEION)

Now you know what an entablature means; suppose we compare the entablatures of our little Greek family. You will find that they differ almost as much as their columns, especially in the frieze and the cornice.

The Ionic and the Corinthian frieze (Fig. 14 and Fig. 15) is one continuous piece of sculpture, while the Doric frieze is broken up into square slabs or panels, called METOPES (Fig. 13). And very lively squares they are! (In this particu- lar frieze.) At least "every other one" is lively: the alternate square has a simple ornament consisting of three grooves or channels, called TRIGLYPHS (Fig. 13).

But we are more interested in the lively squares. There are 92 of them, and no two are alike. (Compare that with any modern building.) They represent a contest which took place at a marriage feast between the Centaurs and the Lapiths, the

FIG. 15. - GREEK CORINTHIAN ENTABLATURE
(MONUMENT OF LYSICRATES)

Centaurs being fabulous creatures, half horse, half human, while the Lapiths are entirely human. Each Metope or slab is a kind of framed picture in stone, representing a single incident in this great contest. The Centaurs seem to be getting the best of it. Here is one carrying off a Lapith woman (Fig. 16). Notice the pointed ears, so characteristic of a low type. Here is another Centaur in the act of crushing his foe with a wine vessel, while the poor victim, in falling, endeavours to protect himself with his shield (Fig. 17).

It is a curious fact that the finest remains of Grecian sculpture represent fabulous events and fabulous animals. These fighting Centaurs, for instance, have been more multiplied than any

FIG. 16. - PARTHENON METOPE

other subject. Perhaps the reason lies partly in the fact that they typify, in a kind of allegory, the first contests between civilisation and barbarism, the Centaurs standing for barbarism and the Lapiths for civilisation.

Ruskin puts it beautifully in one of his books when he says: "The Greeks were the first people that were born into complete humanity. All nations before them had been partly savage — bestial, clay-encumbered: still semi-goat, or semi-ant, or semi-stone, or semi-cloud. But the power of a new spirit came upon the Greeks, and the stones were filled with breath, and the clouds clothed with flesh; and then came the great spiritual battle between the Centaurs and Lapiths, and the living creatures became the CHILDREN OF MEN."

FIG. 17. - PARTHENON METOPE

THE ERECHTHEUM

On the steep rock in Athens called the Acropolis, there stand the remains of two temples made of the purest white marble. Both are Grecian, therefore both beautiful, but with a difference; for the one is Doric, the other Ionic. The one bears throughout the impress of

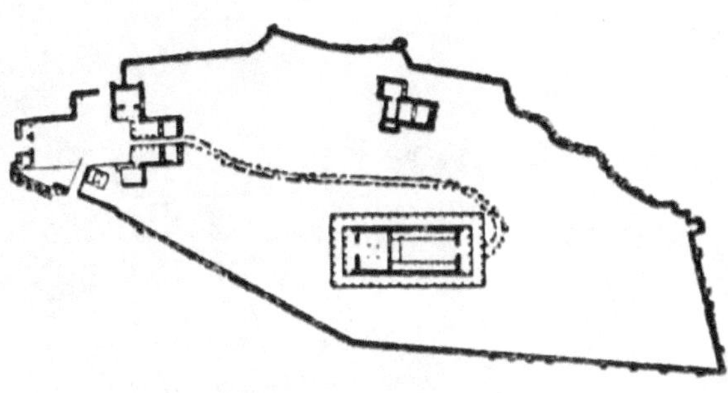

FIG. 18. - PLAN OF ACROPOLIS

repose, solidity, and strength; the other of grace and delicacy. In the one, the columns are short, powerful, and closely ranged together. In the other, they are taller, lighter, and farther apart.

Here is a plan of the Acropolis, with the two temples marked on it (Fig. 18). The big one near the middle is the Parthenon, the most perfect building in all Greece.

But we are going to look first at the other temple, the little irregularly shaped one near the north wall. This is the Erechtheum (Plate I).

The most striking thing about this temple is its irregularity.

The typical Grecian temple consisted of an oblong chamber (the NAOS or CELLA), more or less adorned with columns. According to the number and position of these, the temple received different names. For instance, if the columns entirely surrounded the building, it was called peristyle (Fig. 19). This word is derived from the Greek peri, meaning "around," and stulos, meaning "a column."

PLATE I

THE ERECTHEUM ATHENS, FROM THE WEST
(SEE P. 9)

If, again, the columns were at the two ends only, the temple was said to be amphiprostyle (Fig. 20). (Amphi, meaning "both," and pro, meaning "in front of"—that is, at both fronts.)

FIG. 19. - TEMPLE PLANS

If at one end only, it was prostyle or pronaos (Fig. 21). (Pro, meaning "in front of," and naos, meaning "a temple.")

Such were the commonest forms of a Greek temple, but the Erechtheum was like none of these. It had three porticoes, and two of them in the wrong place from the Greek point of view. Instead of being at the east and west ends, they were east, north, and south. There was a good reason for this, as for everything else the Greeks did.

FIGS. 20 AND 21. - TEMPLE PLANS

You remember what St. Paul said to the Athenians: "I perceive that in all things ye are too superstitious." Had he lived in the days of Pericles, when this temple was built, he might still have had reason to say so, for it was to cover two sacred objects, an olive tree and a salt well, that the Erechtheum was built in this particular way.

I know you are wondering who these graceful women are in the porch. They are called Caryatides (Plate II), and a good name too, for they carry a considerable weight. Some people think it does not look very kind or natural to see women carrying such a heavy burden, but you know women do carry heavy burdens. Some people think they support the whole nation, so why not this little porch?

THE PARTHENON

"Earth proudly wears the Parthenon
As the best gem upon her zone."

You may have seen buildings something like this in your streets (Plate III). The Parthenon, from which they are copied — or rather, on which they are more or less modelled, for there are not many exact copies — is the most perfect building in all Greece, or, as some people think, in the world.

You would not guess that, would you? It all looks so simple: just an oblong apartment, with a colonnade of columns all around, and a double row at the two ends, and a few statues — or the broken fragments of them — in the gables. You almost feel as if you could make a Parthenon yourself! But there you would be mistaken. There is a great deal more in this building than you think. It is the height of art to conceal art, and there is a great deal of concealed art in this simple-looking building. It is a work of genius, the result of infinite labour, skill, knowledge, and pains. Every little bit of it is carefully planned, thought out, and calculated down to the smallest detail. There is not a thing in the whole building you could alter without spoiling the effect — not a change you could make that would not be a change for the worse. You could not add one inch to the height of a column or take away a fraction from its breadth. Everything is calculated; nothing is left to chance. It is not an accident, for instance, that the

CARVATIDE PORCH OF THE ERECHTHEUM, ATHENS
(SEE P. 9)

Parthenon has just forty-six columns, and that the columns are of that particular height and breadth. The Greeks did nothing by accident. They knew that these measurements would produce the best effect and make the most pleasing impression — hence they used them.

There is nothing startling about the Parthenon, or eccentric. Its beauty is of a quiet order — quiet and restful. Everything is orderly, symmetrical, well-balanced, and in perfect proportion. The Greeks knew more about the laws of proportion than any other nation, and it would have pained them to see anything that was out of harmony with these laws. The columns are all of the same height, breadth, and distance from each other (that is what is meant by symmetrical). Its lines are horizontal. No soaring vaults here, nor heaven-aspiring spires, as in the Gothic. It is not stimulating but restful. Its quiet beauty will grow on you. The longer you look, the more you will see in it.

Yes, in it! — that is, in the Parthenon, not in any modern imitation of it. For between the two there is a great gulf fixed. The temple *was* a temple — not a bank or storeroom. It was made of the purest white marble, adorned by the greatest of Grecian sculptors, enriched by colour, and warmed by the glorious sun of Greece. Lastly, it contained one of the two most celebrated statues in the ancient world, that of Athena Parthenos, or the "Virgin Goddess," in whose honour the temple was built. Parthenos means "Virgin" — hence the name Parthenon.

Once upon a time, had you gone inside, you would have seen a colossal gold-and-ivory statue of the goddess, standing nearly forty feet high, with a spear and shield in one hand, a figure of Victory in the other, and the head of the Gorgon Medusa on her breast. This statue was by the world-famous sculptor Pheidias, the same who designed the Parthenon, and was one of the two most celebrated statues in the ancient world. But it is gone now, along with so much else that was the pride and joy of the Greeks.

A FAMOUS FRIEZE

"To copy the form of the Parthenon without its friezes and frontal statuary is like copying a human being without its eyes and mouth."   — RUSKIN

In one of his eloquent books on Art, Ruskin says: "I do with a building as I do with a man — watch the eye and the lips; when they are bright and eloquent, the form of the body is of little consequence."

Now, what does Ruskin mean by the eye and the lips of a building? He just means the painting and sculpture that adorn it, which he considers the principal part because it is the part in which the mind is contained.

The eye and the lips of the Parthenon are its friezes. We saw the frieze of the entablature on this temple, but a frieze is not confined to an entablature. It is the name given to any horizontal band enriched with sculpture, and the frieze we are going to look at now ran all around the temple, on the outside walls or cella, just behind the columns. It was, unfortunately, not in a position to get much light. So, to counteract this defect and give it all the light possible, it was made in very low relief. This means that it does not project much from the wall, scarcely an inch.

You know that flatness gives light, and projection gives shadow. If you want shade on a hot day, you look out for a porch or something that projects, and you avoid the flat wall,

THE PARTHENON, ATHENS
(SEE P. 11)

which gives unbroken light and sunshine. So the Greeks very wisely made this frieze flat, or in low relief, that it might have as much light as possible.

The subject represented is the PANATHENAIC procession — that is, the "ALL ATHENS" procession. Pan is a Greek word for "ALL," and the PANATHENAIC procession was the procession of Athens and all her dependencies, which took place every four years in honour of the goddess "ATHENA". The figures in the frieze are marching to place a sacred veil or mantle (the Peplum) before the statue of the goddess in this very temple. The frieze starts from the southwest angle, running east and north, and meets at the eastern front before the assembled gods, who receive the sacred veil from the hands of the maidens.

On the west front, you see them preparing for the procession. Some are standing by their horses. Others have already mounted and are impatient to start. The fiery, irregular movements of the horses contrast with the firm seats and steady attitudes of the riders. In front of the cavalry are the chariots and charioteers, preceded by the old men carrying the olive branches. Here again, there is a fine contrast between the animation of the chariot groups and the quiet and leisurely walk of the old men. In advance of these is a band of musicians, preceded by the bearers of offerings and, next, the victims for the sacrifice. Here is one — an ox "lowing to the skies" (Plate IV). Poor beast! It is going to be sacrificed in honour of the goddess, but it does not know it and looks quite happy. On the eastern front, you see the maidens who have worked the sacred veil, preceded by a group of magistrates who receive the advancing processions. Between these are twelve seated figures of the gods, and in the centre of all is

BULL, GOING TO SACRIFICE (PARTHENON FREEZE)

(SEE P. 17)

a group which is supposed to represent the offering of the sacred veil to Athena.

Such was this frieze, the longest piece of continuous sculpture in Greece, and the most beautiful in the world. If it had been executed only yesterday instead of two thousand years ago, it would still have been as wonderful and as valuable as it is now. And that for two reasons: firstly, because it is a beautiful work of art, and secondly, because it is an important historical document. It teaches us more and gives us a truer picture of the Athenian people than a hundred treatises; for it sets before us in a way which no mere words can do the very form and spirit of Athens in the age of Pericles.

As a work of art, its surpassing excellence consists in its variety and its vitality. The variety is very striking. There are more than a hundred figures, and no two are alike. They differ in age, in attitude, in action, in form, and in sex. Every class is represented: the charioteer and slave, the stately magistrate

FIG. 22. - PARTHENON FRIEZE

and venerable seer, the victors in their chariots drawn by the steeds which had won for them the priceless garland, the splendid cavalry, the noble youths on their favourite steeds in the flush and pride of their young lives, the train of high-born maidens marching with bowed heads and quiet gait, the gods of Olympus with their priests, and the poor dumb victims which bled upon their altars.

And the vitality is as remarkable as the variety. We can scarcely believe that the figures are not alive. The horses appear to live and move, to roll their eyes, to gallop, prance, and curvet. The veins of their faces and legs seem distended with circulation. It would be interesting to find the secret of this extraordinary vitality. One writer suggests a possible explanation. He says that many of the figures in the frieze owe their charm and vitality to a conflict between two distinct movements, as, for instance, where a rider, while controlling the curvetting of his horse, turns to speak to a comrade behind them (Fig. 22), or where a youth, preparing to take his place in the procession, stoops to bind his sandal and at the same time looks up to watch those who have already started (Fig. 23).

FIG. 23. - PARTHENON FRIEZE

WHY THE GREEKS EXCELLED IN SCULPTURE

"But," it might well be asked, "why were the Greeks such clever sculptors? How is it that they were able to produce statues which are the delight and despair of succeeding generations?"

One reason is that they had so many opportunities of seeing graceful figures that their eyes became trained to beauty of form, and it was only natural that they should produce beautiful forms and produce them with ease. They had not far to go in search of models. They met them everywhere. The Greeks were a nation of athletes. They engaged in all sorts of physical exercises, and, generally speaking, unencumbered by clothing. They had friendly contests in running, wrestling, leaping, boxing, disc-throwing, and by these means their bodies were rendered beautiful and their motions graceful. Then there were the Olympic Games, to which the competitors and spectators thronged from all parts of Greece. The much-coveted prize was a wreath of wild olives, and to gain it the successful competitor had not only to show skill but grace. Think what an impulse all this would be to the art of sculpture!

But there was another influence at work, almost as powerful as the Games, and that was the dancing. Now, you must not suppose that this dancing had anything in common with our modern ballroom dancing or the ballet dancing of the stage. With the Greeks, dancing was not a mere recreation, but a thoughtful and highly intellectual exercise. It aimed at expressing emotion and at telling a story — the story of some old Greek legend. And the story had not only to be clearly, but gracefully and beautifully told; for the dancing was done in public, before a crowd of eager spectators who criticised every false attitude or awkward gesture. The standard was a high one — nothing short of perfection would satisfy. It was a severe school, but a magnificent one. With such a training and such models ever before them, can you wonder that the Greeks became a world-renowned nation of sculptors?

THE PEDIMENTS OF THE PARTHENON

When a person or a nation can do anything particularly well, that person or nation is very fond of doing it, and the Greeks were no exception to this rule. They lost no opportunity of practising their art and of exhibiting it when done. They did not put it under a glass case or into a museum, but on the outside of their temples, where everyone could see it, enjoy it, and be the better for it. Now, look at the Parthenon and see if there is any place that could still be utilised, any little vantage ground or foothold for a statue.

What about the Pediments, those triangular spaces at the east and west front formed by the ends of the roof above the two porticoes? Do you suppose the Greeks would leave them empty as we do? No, indeed! Both pediments were filled with colossal statues of gods and goddesses, of which, however, only mutilated fragments remain, many of them headless, yet priceless. Here is a group known as "The Fates" (Plate V). Not one of the three figures has a head, but how much is expressed by their bodies and their draperies. Each fold has a meaning and a purpose in the general scheme. Then again, all the figures in the pediment are adapted to their position. Those at the angles, such as the first figure in the group of "The Fates," are made lying down; those next to them are in a sitting posture; while those in the centre, where there was most room, stand upright.

THE THREE FATES (PEDINENT OF PARTHENON)
(SEE P. 22)

These figures are not mere isolated statues of gods and goddesses. They tell a story. The eastern pediment represents the birth of Athena, who is supposed to have sprung out of Zeus' head one day when he had a headache. The moment depicted is the one just after her birth. Unfortunately, the figure of Athena is lost, but we can see the other gods and goddesses looking around in amazement, as well they might. When we remember that Zeus is the source and Father of all the gods, and that Athena is the Goddess of Wisdom, we need not wonder that she "came out of his head," as the Greeks thought, and as we say. The other pediment represents the contest between Athena and Poseidon for the land of Attica. It was decided that this land should be given to the one who produced the thing most useful to the citizens, the twelve gods being appointed judges. Poseidon struck the ground with his trident and produced a salt spring, or, according to another version, a horse; while Athena produced an olive tree. The gods decided in favour of the goddess. The scene of this contest was the Acropolis, just where the Erechtheum now stands, and it was to commemorate Athena's victory and mark the spot of the sacred olive tree and salt spring that the Erechtheum was built so irregularly.

THE ELGIN MARBLES

If you live among artists, you will hear them talk lovingly of the Elgin Marbles, and you may wonder what these are.

Well, they are just the very sculptures we have been considering, or the broken fragments of them. For the poor Parthenon had a sad history.

Until two and a half centuries ago, it remained comparatively unchanged, but in 1670, when Athens was besieged by the Turks, a shell exploded in this shrine (which had been turned into a powder magazine), "and instantly, with one wild roar, as though Nature herself were shrieking at the sacrilege, the Parthenon was ruined! Columns on either side were blown to atoms, severing the front of the temple from the rear, and covering the whole plateau with marble fragments, mute witnesses of beauty forever lost to us." But some of those precious fragments were saved from the general wreck, and these are the famous Elgin Marbles.

This is how they got their name.

A Scottish nobleman, named Lord Elgin, was living in Athens about the beginning of the nineteenth century, and such was his admiration for these sculptures that he bought many of them from the Turkish Government for an enormous sum of money and sent them home to Britain in chests. But alas! One of the ships was wrecked, and the precious marbles went to the bottom of the sea, whence, however, they were with difficulty recovered by skilled divers, and, after much tossing to and fro, at last found their way to England and a home in the British Museum.

Here you may see them any day if you are fortunate enough to live in London. If not, you can see casts of them in the Edinburgh Museum and elsewhere.

The Grecian style of architecture is much admired, and you will see examples of it everywhere. In London, for instance, the front of the British Museum is a reproduction of a Grecian temple; and if you live in Edinburgh, you will make some interesting discoveries for yourself of buildings modeled on the Greek. But all these are copies. If you want the genuine article — a real Grecian temple built by Greeks for Greeks — you must go to Greece itself, or to Asia Minor, or to Southern Italy, which, from its numerous Greek colonies, has been called Greater Greece.

CHAPTER II

ROMAN ARCHITECTURE

THE PANTHEON

IT has been well said that there are three Romes: the Rome of the Empire, or Early Rome — The Rome of the Popes, or Medieval, that is, Middle Age Rome; and the Rome of the present day, or Modern Rome.

These three are not apart, but closely associated, side by side, the one touching the other, the one made partly out of the very stones of the other. It is this intermingling of old and new, of ancient ruin and modern palace, that gives the city its lasting and pathetic interest.

At present, we shall confine ourselves to the buildings that belong to Early Rome; and of these, two overtop all the others in importance and interest — the PANTHEON and the COLOSSEUM, a temple and a theater.

The Pantheon (Plate VI) was erected in the reign of Hadrian, the Roman Emperor, and stands to this day almost as perfect as when it was first built, nearly two thousand years ago.

In form, it is a huge round, a perfect circle. This "round-ness" is the most characteristic thing about it. The Romans delighted in the circle. It was their favorite form. They had round buildings, round tops to their doors and windows,

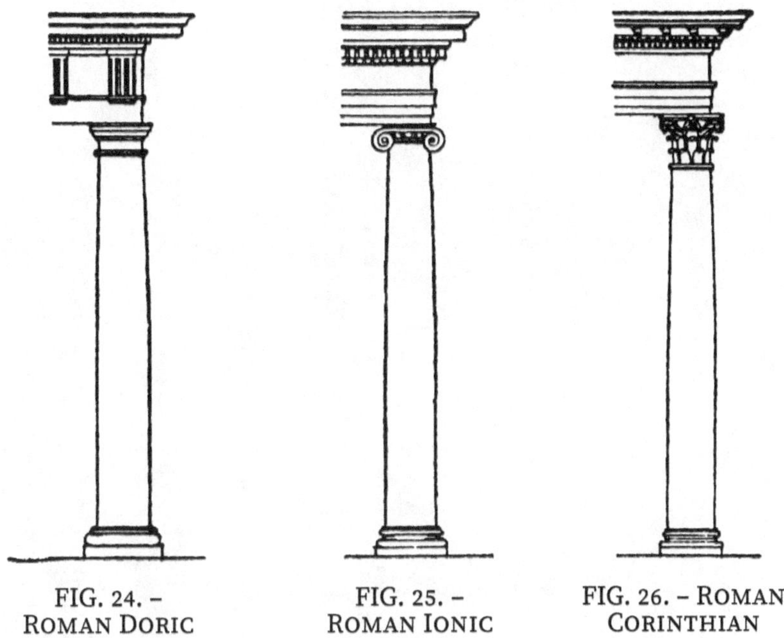

FIG. 24. – ROMAN DORIC

FIG. 25. – ROMAN IONIC

FIG. 26. – ROMAN CORINTHIAN

round arches resting on round pillars, and a round roof crowning all. Such a roof is called a dome or vault.

But what is this?

The "roundness" is broken — and by a Greek portico! It looks strangely out of place here. Both are beautiful — the Greek portico and the Roman temple — but they do not go together.

This portico is not the only thing that the Romans borrowed from the Greeks. If it is true that "imitation is the sincerest flattery," the Greeks ought to feel flattered; for the Romans borrowed all their three "orders" — the Doric, the Ionic, and the Corinthian. But you must not expect to find these "orders" just as we saw them in Greece, in their native simplicity. Few people can leave things exactly the same as they find them, without something added or taken away, and certainly the Romans could not. They altered

THE PANTHEON, ROME
(SEE P. 26)

FIG. 27. PANTHEON NICHE (PIRANESI)

all three "orders" by turn, under the impression that they were improving them. Here are our friends after they have made the acquaintance of the Romans (Figs. 24, 25, and 26).

To these three, the Romans added two other orders of their own — the Tuscan and the Composite, neither of which is very original.

The Tuscan is a kind of shabby Doric, and the Composite is a mixture or compound of the Ionic and the Corinthian. "His name is a brief of his nature," says an old writer quaintly, "for this pillar is nothing but a medley of all the preceding ornaments, making a new kind by stealth, and, though the most richly decked, yet the poorest in this, that he is a borrower of all his beauty."

But all this time, we have been kept waiting in the portico of the Pantheon. Let us go in.

* * * * *

How vast it is, and how silent! Not a sound from the outer world reaches our ears. The loudest street noise would not be heard here. There are no windows, only one huge round hole in the great dome above our head, through which the light streams, making a large circle of sunshine on the marble floor below, and the rain, too, falls, making a great round patch of moisture.

In the walls are eight niches, whose stone arches are supported on yellow marble columns with Corinthian capitals (Fig. 27). In these niches, there once stood the statues of the Olympian gods; but they are now empty, for the Pantheon is no longer a Pagan temple, but a Christian church.

THE TRIUMPHAL COLUMN AND THE TRIUMPHAL ARCH

"See, the conquering hero comes!"

The architecture of Rome is so mixed up with her history that we can scarcely speak of the one without constantly alluding to the other. Here, for instance, was the marketplace or Forum, a place teeming with memories. Yonder stood the rostrum, or orator's pulpit, made of yellow marble and adorned with the prows of ships.

A little farther off was Pompey's statue, at the base of which "great Caesar fell!" In another forum not far off stood the famous Trajan Column — a lofty column with a figure of Trajan at the top and his conquests graven round the shaft. Such a column was peculiarly Roman. The Greek column seldom stood alone. It was always in company, associated with other columns like itself, one of a number. But the Roman column was solitary, with a solitary figure at the top, as lonely as itself. That was the Roman way of honouring a hero. It was supposed to be very gratifying to the hero to see his statue up there.

ARCH OF TITUS, ROME
(SEE P. 32)

Another way of showing honour was by the TRIUMPHAL ARCH.

Two of the most famous of these arches are still standing — the ARCH OF CONSTANTINE, the first Christian Emperor, and the ARCH OF TITUS, the conqueror of Jerusalem.

The Arch of Titus (Plate VII) is covered with statuary. We see the hero entering Rome on a car drawn by four horses, while the Goddess of Victory crowns him with laurels. On the other side of the arch, the spoils of war are being carried in procession—the seven-branched candlestick, the silver trumpet, and the Ark of the Covenant.

Usually, a Roman triumphal arch was triple, but the Arch of Titus is somewhat different.

It has only one big arch and a flat beam above called the "Attic," with columns in front, which seem to support the latter.

Seem only! — for alas, they are not there for use but show! They are decorative, not constructive.

And that is the great difference between Greek art and Roman art, and between all good architecture and the not-so-good. The one takes the useful and proceeds to ornament it. That is constructive. The other uses ornament for ornament's sake. That is decorative.

In the Greek temple, the column is a part of the whole building, almost as much so as the roof itself. In the Roman, it is frequently a mere ornament. If you were to take away a column from the Parthenon, it would topple down; but if you were to abstract one from a Roman building, it would stand as straight as ever: and this, not because of its Spartan-like power of endurance, but because the columns are there for ornament, not use.

THE COLOSSEUM

"I see before me the Gladiator lie."

Not far from the Colosseum, the biggest building in all Rome, was a small round temple with Corinthian columns (Fig. 28). This was the Temple of Vesta, the Goddess of the Hearth.

Within were the white-veiled maidens whose duty it was to keep the sacred fire forever burning. Another duty they had, and a painful one: namely, to attend the gladiatorial combats. They met in that round portico and passed along the Forum to the Colosseum (Plate VIII) where the shows were held, and where we will accompany them.

This building is the most majestic ruin in all Rome. Rows

FIG. 28. - TEMPLE OF VESTA, ROME. (MATER MATUTA.)

THE COLOSSEUM, ROME
(See p. 30)

and rows of ruined arches, supported on magnificent columns and surrounding the immense arena, rise in a gigantic circle towards the sky.

Suppose we examine these columns and find out what "order" they belong to.

But what is this? There is not one order here, but three! — Doric below, Ionic in the middle, and Corinthian above. What a contrast to the Greek buildings we have been looking at! The Parthenon was all Doric, the Erechtheum all Ionic, and the Temple of Zeus all Corinthian. That is what is meant by a Pure Style. But such severe simplicity did not appeal to the Romans. They liked something more ornate and mixed their "orders" without the slightest scruple, and, it must be confessed, sometimes with excellent effect.

You know the uses to which this huge amphitheatre was put? How crowds and crowds of Romans, more than fifty thousand at a time, assembled here to witness the famous gladiatorial combats: that is, the spectacle of men, women, and children, slaves and gladiators, fighting with each other, or with wild beasts, till one or other dropped down dead — "butchered to make a Roman holiday!"

They fought fiercely but hopelessly, for they were at the mercy of a merciless crowd bent on amusement, and their silent appeal for "Pardon" was almost invariably met by the down-turned thumb, which was the signal for the fighting to go on. Their only hope lay in the intercession of the Vestal Virgins, those women we saw in the temple guarding the sacred fire. These would fain have shown mercy and ended the horrible butchery, but they feared to disappoint the multitude, who had come to see the sport and would not be baulked.

Sometimes there were Christians among the victims. They were not afraid to die, for they were dying for their faith and gloried in their martyrdom. Before the struggle, they used to greet the Emperor with the words, "Ave! Caesar! morituri te salutant" ("Hail Caesar! Those about to die salute thee!").

But there were others who had not their faith to sustain them, and who felt very bitterly towards their Roman oppressors. In a famous piece of sculpture, called "The Dying Gladiator," we see one of these — a Dacian, whose home is far away on the Danube. He is thinking, as he dies, of his wife and little ones, widowed and fatherless, and his thoughts are very bitter as he wonders at the cruelty of it all.

This statue is in Rome, and the verse which follows is from Lord Byron's poem on the same subject:

> "The arena swims around him — he is gone,
> Ere ceased the inhuman shout which hailed the
> wretch who won.
> He heard it, but he heeded not — his eyes
> Were with his heart, and that was far away;
> He recked not of the life he lost nor prize,
> But where his rude hut by the Danube lay,
> There were his young barbarians all at play,
> There was their Dacian mother — he, their sire,
> Butchered to make a Roman holiday —
> All this rushed with his blood — shall he expire,
> And unavenged? Arise! ye Goths, and glut your ire!"

ROMAN GENIUS

> "Rome, proud mistress of the world,
> Tramples on a thousand states."

The Romans were the greatest builders the world has ever seen. Their temples, palaces, theatres, roads, bridges,

FIG. 29. - BRIDGE OVER ST. MARTIN, AOSTA

walls, fortifications, and aqueducts are world-famous and seem as if they were built to endure forever. You will see examples of them in all parts of the world; for wherever the Romans conquered, they taught their style of building to the conquered nation. How they did it all is the marvel, but there is no doubt about the fact, for many of these edifices stand to this day, a monument to the genius and industry of the men who raised them.

Everything the Romans did was on a gigantic scale. When you walk along a Roman road, it is as if you were walking on the top of a wall, about five feet broad and five feet deep — just broad enough for a chariot.

Their bridges were as famous as their roads (Fig. 29). They always had the semi-circular arch and were strong and massive. You will see many examples of them in Britain; but every bridge with a semi-circular arch is not Roman — many of the so-called Roman bridges are just modern copies.

FIG. 30 - PONT DU GARD, NISMES

You have heard of the Roman aqueducts which were made to bring water from one place to another. Here is a grand one, with its two stories of vaulted arches. The water passed over the topmost arches (Fig. 30).

One writer tells how, during a campaign, a girl in the Sabine Mountains gave the general a draught of excellent water. Immediately, the spring from which the water was taken was carried to Rome by an aqueduct forty miles long, which remains to this day firm and solid.

The Romans were marvels in their own way, but it was not a Greek way. They did not go in for subtlety but size — for strength, rather than simplicity. Everything they did was on a colossal scale. The vault of heaven became the model for their arch, the dome for their roof. Their temple, the Pantheon, is dedicated "To All the Gods!"

Their decoration is on an equal scale of magnificence. They did not believe in "Beauty unadorned," but in beauty with all her jewels on at once. Their ornament is lavish. It reminds one of some wealthy matron with a love of sparkling, who covers herself with a profusion of jewels without much care for their fitness.

Still, this goodly matron has many admirers. Byron worshipped her; Shelley immortalised her in his exquisite poem, "Adonais," and poor Keats was content to die in her arms. Her jewels are tarnished now, and their glory faded, but even in decay she is grander than many another in splendour, for, with all her faults, Rome is Rome still.

> "Rome, Rome! thou art not now
>   As thou hast been!
> On thy seven hills of yore
>   Thou sat'st a queen.
>
> Thou hadst thy triumphs then
>   Purpling the street;
> Leaders and sceptred men
>   Bowed at thy feet.
>
> They that thy mantle wore,
>   As gods were seen —
> Rome, Rome! thou art no more
>   As thou hast been!"

CHAPTER III

BYZANTINE ARCHITECTURE

EARLY BYZANTINE—ST. SOPHIA, CONSTANTINOPLE

"In front the Church of Saint Sophia glows,
A pile of jewels set in burnished snows."

THE Byzantine is an architecture of domes, and its chief seat is at Constantinople.

I hope you remember that the old name for Constantinople is Byzantium, or you will wonder why this style should be called "Byzantine," and not "Constantinople-ine!"

The ancient town of Byzantium was almost in ruins when the Emperor Constantine chose it for the new capital of the Roman Empire. He rebuilt the city and named it after himself, Constantinople. Here he erected a magnificent church to St. Sophia, or "The Holy Wisdom," but this was unfortunately burnt to the ground, and the present Church of St. Sophia (Plate IX) was erected two centuries later on the same spot, by the Emperor Justinian.

It is difficult to speak of this marvellous building without appearing to exaggerate, but I must try to give you some idea of its magnificence.

The ground plan is a SQUARE — not an exact square, for it

INTERIOR OF SAINT SOPHIA, CONSTANTINOPLE
(*See p. 40*)

is broken in front by a PORTICO and TWO ENTRANCE COURTS, and at the back by an apse, or rounded recess.

The outer court is itself a SQUARE, surrounded by arcades (see p. 49), and with a fountain in the middle, the symbol of purification.

The inner court is for penitents.

The square is repeated in the interior, where four massive piers, connected by four round arches, carry the great central dome. Saint Sophia is thus a square within a square.

You have not heard the word "pier" before. It is a mass of masonry acting as a support — a kind of giant pillar, but with this difference: a pillar is always made either of one stone, or in courses of single stones, while a pier may be built up of a number of little stones.

St. Sophia is a mass of DOMES. It is crowned in the centre by a huge dome of glittering gold, and numbers of smaller domes and semi-domes lead up to this central dome, producing a marvellous effect (Fig. 31). These domes are not quite like the Italian ones. Compare St. Sophia with the Roman Pantheon, and you will see two great differences. Firstly, the Roman dome is carried over a ROUND space, while the Byzantine dome is carried over a SQUARE space — a much more difficult matter. But there is another difference. The Roman dome is quite round, a perfect hemisphere; while the St. Sophia domes are like our earth, "slightly flattened at the poles," as if somebody had been sitting on them, which certainly has a very flattening effect.

After the domes, the most striking thing about St. Sophia is its COLOUR.

Now, colour is a great magician. It can make a cottage seem a palace. If you doubt that, go and visit a place on a dull day, and then go again when the sun is shining and bringing out all

FIG. 31. SAINT SOPHIA

the different hues and tints. You will scarcely believe that you are looking at the same scene. There are many ways of getting colour in a building. You might paint its walls, or you might hang up pictures on them, or put in stained glass windows, or you might cover the walls with damask, or with variegated marbles of every hue — and this last is the Byzantine method. It is called MOSAIC and is a kind of painting with scraps of marble or glass. The effect is both beautiful and lasting, far more so than any other kind of decoration; as witnessed in St. Sophia, which shines like an Aladdin's palace. The walls and pillars, and even the floor of this temple, are inlaid with precious stones, gold, and jewels of every hue, while the vaults are covered with mosaics on a ground of gold. The whole interior glitters and glimmers with the most varied play of colour. "One might believe," says an old writer, "that the inner space is not lighted from without by the sun at all, but that radiance dwells actually within it, so vast a flood of light pours itself throughout this House of God."

THE BUILDING OF ST. SOPHIA

A LEGEND

There is a quaint legend in connection with the building of this church. The story goes that the great Justinian, Emperor of Byzantium, looking around his city, and seeing no worthy temple, said within himself:— "I shall build a temple to the Eternal Wisdom and the Eternal Truth; one that shall surpass in magnificence all other temples that ever were built. Within, all shall be of dazzling magnificence. Cherubs and seraphs of many-colored stones shall encircle the King of Kings, and on either hand will stand the Twelve Apostles. And above all, the face of the Saviour, calm and majestic, will look down from a nimbus set with jewelled rays. Solomon took gifts for his temple, but I shall build mine alone and unaided. None shall share the cost; none divide the glory. My name alone shall be graven above the portal as sole giver."

So Justinian sent for an artist, the greatest of his age, and said:—

"Build me a temple to the Eternal Wisdom and the Eternal Truth. Build it of the best — best style, best materials, best workmanship. Let none contribute to it, none share the cost, none divide the glory. And above the portal, engrave in letters of gold:

'This House to God, Justinian, Emperor, gave.'
In the name of Wisdom, build."

For seven long years, the workmen labored at their task. Stone upon stone they laid, arch upon arch, column on column, pier above pier, till at last the pile was complete, and the temple rose into the air — walls, roof, pillars, portals, and, crowning all, the mighty dome, which, "white as mountain snow, hangs like a moon above the second Rome."

And now the great day has arrived — the day for which Justinian longed, prayed, and waited — the day of his triumph.

The crowds poured in on every side, and thronged the temple. In their midst, his head higher than all the rest, came the Emperor. Proudly, he glanced round, with an "alone-I-did-it" look on his haughty countenance, while his eye eagerly sought the marble slab on which his name and deed were graven.

But what is this?

With an angry gesture, he started back, for there, instead of the expected words, he read:

"This House to God, Euphrasia, widow, gave."

Trembling with rage, he summoned his sculptor and, pointing to the offending words, cried:

"What does this mean? Thou wilt pay dear for thy ill-timed jest."

"Pardon, Sire!" cried the sculptor, as he threw himself prostrate at the feet of the monarch. "But I know nothing of this! That is not the name I carved above the portal."

"It is false!" said Justinian. "Do not add a lie unto thy guilt."

Then an old man, a priest, came forward and said — "He speaks true, O King! I saw him carve thy name. Some other hand hath done this: the hand, perchance, that wrote the Tables of the Law on Mount Sinai, the hand that wrote Belshazzar's doom on the walls of his palace."

"Oh, indeed!" jeered the monarch. "I thought the age of miracles was passed. Who, then, is this woman, this widow Euphrasia, who has dared to disobey my commands and stolen the honour due to me? Bring her before me."

But no one knew any such woman.

At last, an old man came forward and said — "There is one of that name who lives near the quay, but she is old, and lame, and feeble, and very poor, and could not possibly have built this temple."

"Find her!" shouted the monarch. "Bring her before me."

So the messenger went out in search of the widow Euphrasia, and the people waited in the temple in hushed silence.

After some hours, they returned, bringing with them an old woman, scantily clothed, and leaning on a stick.

"Euphrasia!" said Justinian sternly, "how hast thou dared to disobey my commands and contribute to the building of this temple? Speak."

Then the poor woman faltered -

"Pardon, O King! But I did not mean to offend. I only gave a little straw to the oxen that drew the heavy wagons of marble for thy temple. For I had been ill for months, and one day a little bird came and sat on my window-sill and sang so sweetly that I thought the Lord of Heaven had sent it on purpose to comfort me. And my heart was full of love to the good God who had sent me this little comforter, and I longed to do something in return. Just then, the wagons passed, laden with marbles for this temple, so I pulled a little straw out of my mattress and gave it to the beasts that were dragging the carts. That is all!"

Then, at last, the scales fell from Justinian's eyes, and he knew why his proud gift had been rejected and the poor woman's gift of love accepted.

CHAPTER IV

ROMANESQUE ARCHITECTURE

ROMANESQUE — WHAT IS IT?

YOU have never heard of the Romanesque before — at least not in this book — and you probably think it is something very far away; and so it is, but it is also very near — "so near and yet so far" — as the song says. For the Romanesque has several names, and one of its names is Norman! The reason for these different names is that this style was practiced in many countries besides its native land, and it got a different name in each country. In Germany, it was called Rhenish; in France, Romane; in England and Scotland, Norman; and in Italy, its native land, it had two names — Lombard and Tuscan. These do not all mean quite the same thing. There is a good deal of difference between the Romanesque of Lombardy and the Romanesque of Tuscany, and still more between the Romanesque of Italy and that of France and Germany. And no wonder. Each country has its own character, and the style of its architecture partakes of that character. But there is another reason for these differences and varieties. The Romanesque style lasted about 800 years (from the fourth to the twelfth century, roughly speaking), and it would be strange if it did not develop some changes in that time. One can do a good deal in 800 years!

But why did the Romanesque style flourish in so many different countries — in France, and Germany, and Spain, and Britain, and over all Western Europe generally?

Well, the reason is that this style is founded on the old Roman, and its originators, the Romans, when they conquered a nation, taught that nation to build in their way, and that way was a Romanesque way. Perhaps you think it should just be called "Roman" at once, and not have a new name and such a long one too. But that would not do at all; for the Romanesque is not the same thing as the old Roman, though it was modelled on the latter, and has many features in common with it, such as the:—

Round arch, with horizontal beam,

Round column,

Round-arched arcade,

and sometimes, especially in baptisteries — round walls. (A baptistery is a place where people are baptized.)

But along with all that, it has something that is not Roman at all — that is in striking contrast to the Roman; something that it got from another source altogether, a northern or Teutonic source; and this "mixture" of North and South is a very pleasant one.

Perhaps the best definition of Romanesque would be — "A Christian Roman." (See Plate X.)

THE BASILICA

The history of the Romanesque is such a long story that I scarcely know where to begin. I should have to go back to those early centuries (which can be expressed in three figures), when Christianity was not yet established and the people who professed it — early Christians, as they are called

CATHEDRAL AND LEANING TOWER, PISA
(See pp. 48, 55, 71)

— had to worship secretly in vaults, tombs, and catacombs. These last are vast underground caverns, which can be seen to this day, in and near Rome, stretching for miles and miles, like a great underground city. Constantine was the first Roman Emperor who openly professed Christianity, and it must have been a grand day for the early Christians when he came to the throne as sole Emperor (in 323 A.D.) and issued an edict that Christianity was to be the state religion. Now, at last, they could come out of their hiding places and worship openly. When they had money enough to build places of worship, they took as their model the basilica, or Roman court of justice (used also as a hall of exchange), and we must stop here and take a good look at this building, because it became the forefather or ancestor of many of our modern churches (Fig. 32).

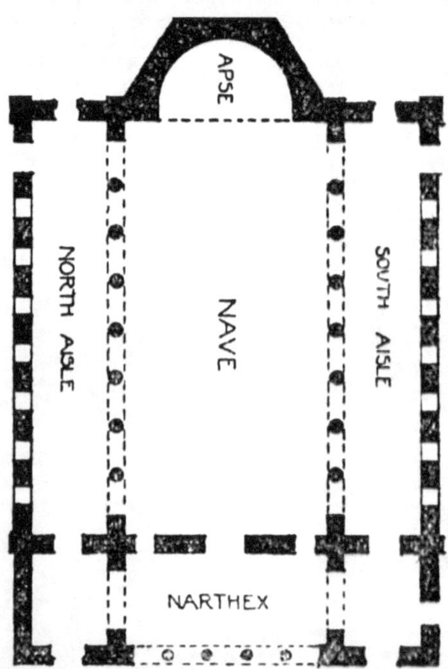

FIG. 32. - BASILICA PLAN ST. JOHN STUDION, CONSTANTINOPLE

In form, the basilica was very simple, just an oblong hall, with a rounded recess at the far end, called an apse.

Two rows of columns, carrying round arches, divided the hall into three parts: a NAVE and two AISLES; or, if there were a double row of columns, a nave and four aisles.

The walls of the nave were higher than those of the aisles,

and high up in them was a row of round-headed windows known as the CLEARSTORY windows. (This word is often spelt clerestory.)

In the rounded recess, or apse, at the east end, was a stone bench, on which the judge sat while deciding cases, and in front of him stood an altar, where sacrifices were offered to the pagan gods.

When the early Christians took the Roman basilica as a model for their churches, they retained the name, giving it, however, a new meaning. "Basilica" means "House of the King," and by "King," the Romans meant the judge, but the Christians meant Christ, who is "King of Kings."

THE SANCTUARY

CROSS AND SCREEN

Now you will understand that when people talk of "a noble basilica," they mean, or ought to mean, a church of this particular form — that is, one modelled on the old Roman court of justice; and if you look around you, you will find that many of the churches you know are of this form.

Not exactly, however. Though the Roman basilica is our common ancestor, it would scarcely recognize its descendants; for we have wandered far from its ways and grown some new features, which we, at any rate, consider improvements. So that, if you were to visit an old Roman basilica (Plate XI) and compare it with the interior of a modern basilican church (which you will probably have an opportunity of doing next Sunday morning, about 11 A.M.), you would notice some big differences; perhaps, indeed, you would be more struck by the difference than by the likeness.

INTERIOR OF ST. PAUL'S –OUTSIDE THE WALLS, ROME

(See p. 51)

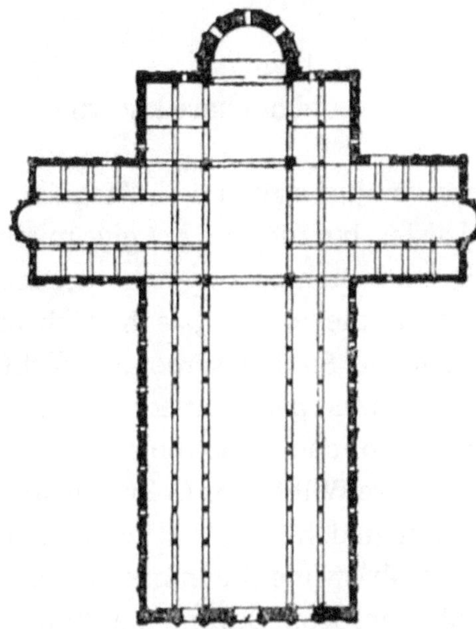

FIG. 33. - PISA CATHEDRAL

That there should be these differences is quite natural. Nothing in the world stands still; progress and movement are the law of life. As the Christian Church grew and prospered, the building, too, grew in dignity and importance.

If you look at this plan of Pisa Cathedral (Fig. 33), (one of the best examples of the later Romanesque), you will see two new features, namely: the TRANSEPT and the CHANCEL.

The first of these is the most important because it altered the form of the building from a simple oblong into a cross, the symbol of Christianity. Not a Greek cross, with all its sides equal, but a Latin cross, which has one long and one short member. "Trans" is the Latin for "across," and you see how the transept runs right across the nave.

After the transept came another important change, the addition of a choir or chancel. This is the part next to the apse, and it was got by prolonging the east end of the nave, raising it on steps, and separating it from the rest of the building by a screen.

A screen is a very useful thing, though I don't suppose it will appeal much to you. Its chief use is for privacy, and boys and girls do not seem particularly anxious for that. But there are times when a screen is almost a necessity, as, for example, in the case of the school where four classes were being taught in one big room! I don't know what the masters would have done without their screen. They would not have known what class they were in.

Now the basilican church was just a great hall. The pillars divided it up into nave and aisles, but they did not give much privacy — not sufficient for the worshippers — who wanted a part separated from the rest of the building, as the Holy of Holies is in the Jewish synagogue. So they screened off the east end — that is, the apse, and the part immediately next to it, which they named chancel or choir. You remember the chancel in Melrose Abbey, where William of Deloraine and the monk of St. Mary's Aisle watched through that awful night to "win the treasure of the tomb," while the monk told William stories of the wizard, Michael Scott. Beyond the choir or chancel was the apse, where the judge used to sit in the old days when the basilica was a court of justice, and where the bishop and clergy now sat. The altar, too, was there, just as in olden times, but over it was a beautiful canopy, and its flames no longer rose "To an Unknown God."

Such is the origin of the "sanctuary."

Having got their "separated portion," the Romanesque architects proceeded to beautify and adorn it — varying the details, decorating, enlarging, and refining, carving a cross here and a capital there — till at last this corner became the most beautiful in the whole church, a shrine within a shrine. What a world of love and devotion it represents! How many precious boxes of alabaster have been poured out on its altars! Each brought his gift — the painter his picture, the sculptor his statue, the Marys their altar-cloth. Whatever of worth or beauty the church possesses will be found here. It draws the eye to it like a magnet. It has been well named THE SANCTUARY.

ARCADES

We have seen "the beauty of the Sanctuary," which attracted to itself the chief ornament of the building, but you must not suppose that the rest of the church was left

FIG. 34. - INTERLACING ARCADE, LEUCHARS, FIFESHIRE

bare and unadorned. The doors and windows were beautifully carved, and the walls were decorated in various ways, the most popular being the Arcade.

An arcade is a long series of arches supported on pillars. The Romanesque builders knew the value of the arcade as a decorative feature, and they covered their walls with them. In Central Italy especially — Florence, Pisa, etc. — the churches are just a mass of arcades (see Plate X). But these arcades are not all true arcades. Some are blind arcades, that is, sham ones, just there for

FIG. 35

ornament. You cannot walk under them because the pillars are attached to the wall.

To this class belong the interlacing arcades, in which the arches seem to go through each other (Fig. 34), and the tiny arcades at the very top of the building, which are sometimes called corbel tables, because they spring from a funny head called a corbel (Fig. 35).

A ST. CATHERINE WINDOW

The Romanesque churches were not entirely dependent on arcades, however, for their decoration: color played an important part. Their walls were adorned with frescoes and variegated marbles. "Fresco" is the method of painting on a wall surface while the plastering is still wet, so that the color penetrates into the interior. You will see two beautiful and interesting examples of frescoes in Plates XII and XIII. Unfortunately, these frescoes are more beautiful than lasting. Time has set his seal on them — his seal and his stain — and many of them have faded away.

But the marble remains beautiful as ever — white marble, green serpentine, red porphyry, royal purple. They are set like jewels into the brickwork and "thrown like a silver girdle or necklace of precious stones round the apse."

From these marble walls, a circular window looks down on the worshipper like a great eye, as round and big as the eye of the Cyclops, and much more beautiful. The giant's eye was in the center of his forehead, and this, the eye of the cathedral, is usually in the center of its west front or principal façade. Sometimes it shines with a gentle radiance, sometimes with dazzling splendor. It all depends on the glass — whether it is pure white, or stained and dyed in all

FRESCO BY GOZZOLI – THE JOURNEY OF THE MAGI
(SEE P. 56)

FRESCO IN GHIRLANDUO – THE BIRTH OF THE VIRGIN, IN
THE CHURCH OF STA. MARIA NOVELLA, FLORENCE

(SEE P. 56)

the colors of the rainbow. From the center of the eye, there radiate spokes as well as sparks, like the spokes of a wheel. Hence, it is sometimes called a "wheel window" (Plate XIV) or a St. Catherine Window (yet another name is rose window).

You know the story of St. Catherine and her wheel?

This good and learned lady had the misfortune to offend some heathen philosophers by defeating them in an argument, and in revenge, they bound her to a wheel armed with spikes, which, at every turn of the machine, pierced her flesh. But one day, her cords were miraculously broken, and St. Catherine was released from her martyrdom.

THE CLOISTER

Sometimes in your wanderings into the country, you come across an old abbey, outside the walls of which are the remains of a beautiful arcade, with broken arches and pillars, and a square space in the middle, overgrown with weeds and shrubs.

That is an old CLOISTER. For the origin of the cloister, we must go back to the Roman house, which was entered by a square court called an ATRIUM.

The Roman Basilica (or Court of Justice) was also entered by an atrium, and when the early Christians took the Basilica as a model for their church, they borrowed the atrium also as a form of approach.

In the Roman Basilica and in the Early Christian Church, the atrium occupied the principal or west front, but after a time, the Christian atrium deserted its position and found a much better one on the south side, where it got all the sun, and where it now appeared under the new name of CLOIS-TERS. It has never changed its name or place since.

WHEEL WINDOW IN CHURCH OF ST. MARY, TUSCANIA, ITALY
(*See p. 59*)

Now you will understand that by a cloister is meant a court, usually square, with arcades all around and a garden in the middle.

Here the monks walked and talked, worked, played, and dreamed. And a more charming place for their working and dreaming could not be found; for, apart from the delights of a garden, there was the arcade, with its long succession of pillars and arches. You remember the arcades we saw on the cathedral walls. Some of these were blind arcades. But the cloister arcades are different — they are the real thing. You can walk under them or rest on their cool flags and watch the dance of the leaves in the cloister garden. Not the merriest little imp of fairyland can dance like them. They seem to know a hundred steps and to learn a new one every minute.

Among the most beautiful cloisters in the world are those of Arles in France (see Plate XVI) and Tarragona in Spain, and the cloisters of St. John Lateran in Rome (Plate XV). But you can see beautiful cloisters nearer home — at Westminster, for instance, and Gloucester.

Sometimes you will come across a lovely old cloister in the most unexpected place, some quiet out-of-the-way village perhaps, with half a dozen houses in it. That was the delightful experience of a thirteen-year-old friend of mine, who was touring with her parents in the south of France when she came to a tiny hamlet, where you would never expect to see fine architecture, and suddenly —

But I think you would like to hear her description of the unexpected cloister in her own words. She says —

"It was a hot day, and we had been motoring all morning when we stopped to admire a church on the road, attracted by the huge carved pillars. It was rather nice inside, but nothing unusual, and we were turning away disappointed when a priest came up. He looked at us a long time but had not made up his mind to talk when I caught sight of a picture of Mary and Jesus. I forgot all about the priest, and simply stood and gazed. It was the frame I was looking at, which was so beautifully carved. Suddenly, I felt a hand on my arm, and heard a voice saying:—

" 'La petite demoiselle likes carving. Perhaps she would like to see the — the —' He did not know the word for cloister but pointed to a door. We opened it and looked out, and oh! how beautiful it was! The cloister was square, and it was made of marble, all worked. The ground you walked on was marble and was worked with pictures of Jesus' life. The walls next to the church were marble and were painted with more scenes from His life. The pillars also were white marble and were worked with the lives of the saints; and on the roof was a long cross, with a carved figure of Jesus on it. And then, if you looked through between the white marble pillars, you saw a garden of red roses, some of them twining around the pillars. In the middle of the garden was another cross with a figure of Jesus on it, and the roses had been trained so as to hang on the cross and twine round and round it without growing on Jesus. The white and red was such a lovely contrast; I could have looked forever."

I think we should all like to see these cloisters with their red roses and white marble pillars.

LAW AND ORDER

We have seen how the Romanesque inherited from its Roman ancestor the round arch, the round column, the round-arched arcade, and its general form — an oblong or a round.

CLOISTERS OF ST. JOHN LATERAN, ROME
(SEE P. 61)

But along with all that, it inherited something else — a mental quality: namely, the Roman love of law and order. The Romans had always submitted gladly to law, and it was only natural that their architecture should bear the stamp of law. The squares of their battalions were not marshaled with more orderliness and discipline than the squares of their cathedrals. Nothing was haphazard, nothing left to chance. All was orderly, measured, and regulated. If you visit a typical Romanesque cathedral, you will see that the space where nave and transept cross each other forms a square. Take note of that square: you will meet it again and again. Here it is in the chancel. Here it is in the transept or arms of the cross. Here it is again, four or five times repeated, in the nave; while smaller squares, just one-fourth the size, compose the side aisles, which are themselves exactly half the width of the nave.

Law and order everywhere!

Such was the Romanesque minster in its early days — sober, dignified, reasonable;

and marked by a repose almost as profound as that which reigned in the palace of the Sleeping Beauty.

Then came a change.

A new spirit crept in, or rather rushed in, disturbing the classic calm and leaving its mark in a form so palpable, and at the same time so picturesque, that we cannot choose but see and admire.

THE MARK OF THE NORTH

You remember what happened to Italy in the fifth century? How hordes and hordes of barbarians swept down on it from the north, ravaging the country, taking Rome, and almost extinguishing the empire? Well, out of evil came forth good, architecturally speaking, for it is to these very barbarians that we owe much that is picturesque in the later Romanesque — that element of romance, of poetry, which gives this style its peculiar charm, and makes it a kind of halfway house between the old Roman and the Gothic.

It is easy to trace the Northern influence, which shows itself chiefly in three ways:

> First, by a rude decoration, quaint but effective.
> Secondly, by grotesque sculptures.
> Thirdly, by towers.

We will look at these in turn, beginning with the quaint decoration. Here are some examples. These mouldings, as they are called, will seem very familiar to you because you have seen them so often on your own churches and Norman castles. They consist of simple line patterns, which are generally massed together, giving a rich, striking effect in spite of their simplicity.

The one you will meet with most often is the Chevron or Zigzag, which sometimes meanders all over the face of the building and sometimes concentrates itself on the doors and windows (Fig. 36). Here it is again in very strange company (Fig. 36A).

Another favourite moulding is the Diamond or Lozenge (Fig. 37). Then there is the Cable (Fig. 38), so called from its resemblance to a rope; the Billet (Fig. 39); the Scallop (Fig. 40); the Double Cone, which looks like two cones placed end-to-end (Fig. 41); and a moulding in imitation of trellis work, something like a basket (Fig. 42).

Have you noticed how few of these lines are straight? They all seem to slant in one direction or another (Fig. 43). Now, that is very suggestive.

CLOISTERS AT ARLES, FRANCE
(See p. 61)

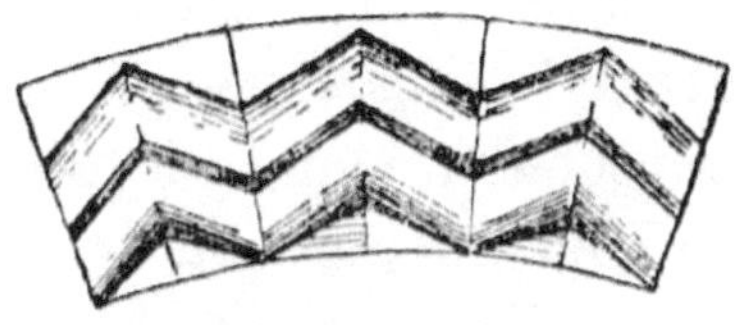

FIG. 36

FIG. 36A. - LINCOLN CATHEDRAL, WEST DOOR

FIG. 37

FIG. 38

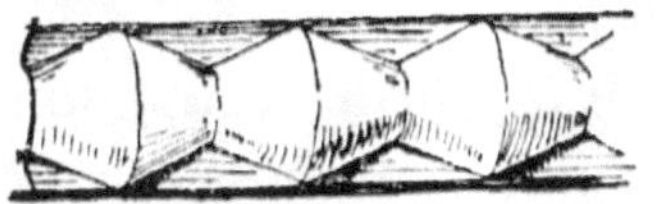

FIG. 39

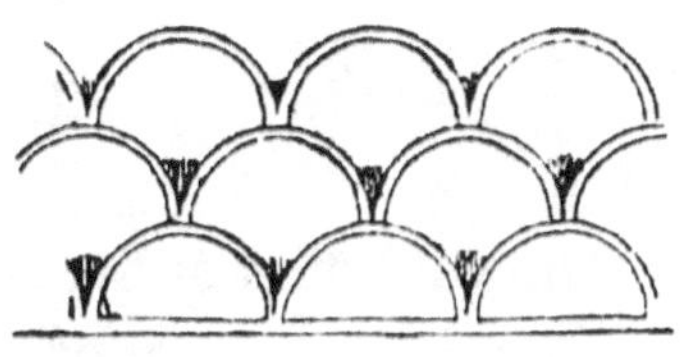

FIG. 40

FIG. 4I

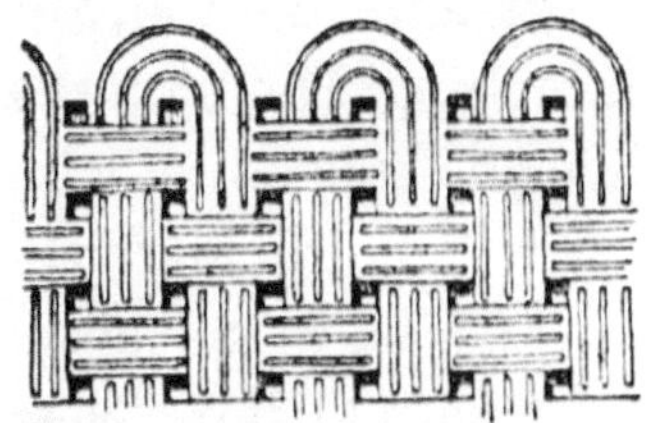

FIG. 42

"Of what?" you ask. Of their Northern origin.

Neither the Greeks nor the Romans used diagonal lines if they could help it. They believed in straight lines. These might be horizontal or vertical, but they must be straight. They preferred the horizontal to every other kind, but they could not always have horizontal lines: they were obliged to use vertical lines sometimes. Well, then, they must be quite vertical, not tumbling to one side or another.

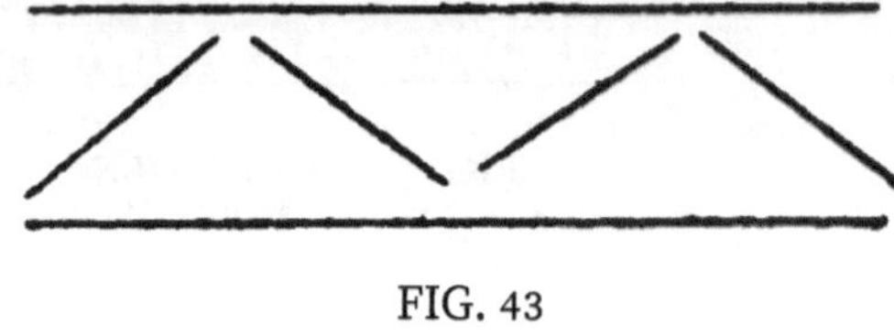

FIG. 43

But these Northerners were different. Straight lines did not appeal to them. They liked everything on the cross. So they covered the face of the building with diagonal lines. They put them on their doors and windows; they carved them on the capitals of their columns; and they wound them in spirals round the shafts.

GROTESQUES

The wild men of the North who conquered Italy did not confine their decoration by any means to diagonal lines or any other kind of line. They gave us something much more exciting — figures of beasts, men, and monsters, all in a very lively frame of mind, and always in action. The action is the main thing. The figures are often rudely cut, but they are all alive and exceedingly busy (Fig. 44).

It is not difficult to guess what their favourite occupation was. "We are in the fair hunting fields of the Lucchese mountains," says Ruskin, "with horse, and hound, and hawk; and merry blast of trumpet. Very strange creatures to be hunted,

DOORWAY OF ST. MICHAELS (ST. MICHELE), PAVIA
(SEE P. 70)

in all truth. Here is the doorway of a church (St. Michele of Pavia), whose walls are covered with figures of apes, and wolves, and mermaids with two tails, and griffins, and dragons without end, or with a dozen of ends, as the case may be."

This kind of sculpture is called GROTESQUE, which means strange or fantastic.

FIG. 44. - S. MICHELE, LUCCA HUNTING FIGURES

Now, all this is in strong contrast to the classic and to the Byzantine.

The East never laughs; or at least it does not put its laughter into its architecture. All there is solemn and austere. But the "Later Romanesque" is simply bubbling over with fun. It is as full of mirth and mischief as a schoolboy on holiday, and as refreshing. This love of play it inherited from its Northern parent. And a good thing too that it did so. The classic alone would be too cold, just as the Teutonic (or Northern) alone would be rather uncouth; but together, they make a perfect whole.

And now, we come to the last of the "Marks of the North," the last and biggest — namely,

THE TOWER

What would our castles and cathedrals be without their tower? We are so familiar with this feature that we can scarcely think of a time when it was not. There is something in the very name. It has romance in it and strength. When Tennyson wished to honour the Duke of Wellington, he compared him to a tower:

"O fall'n at length that Tower of Strength
Which stood four-square to all the winds that blew."

Well, these towers, which added so much to the pictur-esqueness of our castles and cathedrals, we owe to the barbar-ians who swooped down on Italy. After their arrival, towers sprang up on every hand — long towers, short towers, square towers, round towers, octagonal towers. They crowned the centre of the building. They flanked the front like sentinels. They ranged themselves in groups at the far end. In Italy, they detached themselves proudly from the rest of the building and stood apart as "Campanili," or Bell Towers (Plate XVIII).

These towers are not all alike. They vary in character according to their uses.

The Belfry is a peaceful tower, which we associate with Sabbath chimes. It will probably appeal more to you later on when you are older and know the charm of old associations.

The Military Tower is more exciting: it is there for pur-poses of defence. You will see many examples of this kind of tower in England and Scotland, where it was a sad necessity.

Ireland, too, is particularly rich in Military Towers.

Then, there is the Watch Tower, which is closely associ-ated with the Military Tower, its chief use being to keep a look-out on the enemy. It is sad that we should have enemies. Perhaps, someday, when we are angels, or very nearly so, and never, never quarrel, we may not need these Watch Towers, and then we can turn them all into Bell Towers. But in the meantime, seeing that we do have enemies, it is perhaps as well that we should have these Watch Towers to see what they are about.

Some of the most picturesque towers in the world are in Germany. I am not thinking just now of the cathedral towers, which are very striking, but of the castle towers. If you want

CAMPANILE AND ST. MARK'S VENICE
(SEE P. 71)

to know how much these add to the beauty of the landscape (and how much the landscape adds to their beauty), you must take a sail down the Rhine and see the German castles. You will want to get out your sketchbook.

Childe Harold took that sail and was enchanted with the scene. When he came home, he wrote a poem about it, which is so vivid it makes you feel as if you were there and looking on. Here are two of the verses:

I

"The castled crag of Drachenfels
Frowns o'er the wide and winding Rhine,
Whose breast of waters proudly swells
Between the banks which bear the vine
And hills all rich with blossom'd trees,
And fields which promise corn and wine,
And scatter'd cities crowning these,
Whose far white walls along them shine,
Have strew'd a scene which I should see
With double joy wert thou with me."

II

"And peasant girls, with deep blue eyes,
And hands which offer early flowers,
Walk smiling o'er this paradise;
Above, the frequent Feudal Towers
Through green leaves lift their walls of gray,
And many a rock which steeply lowers
And noble arch in proud decay
Look o'er this vale of vintage bowers."

CHAPTER V

NORMAN ARCHITECTURE

A STURDY STYLE

"With massive arches broad and round,
That rose alternate, row on row,
On ponderous columns, short and low."

MARMION.

NOW at last we have crossed the Channel and are on British ground, for the Romanesque is just the Italian name for our own familiar Norman.

Are you wondering why this should be so? Have you forgotten William the Conqueror, who came over from Normandy in 1066 and, among other things, taught us the Norman style of architecture? There had been a little building in that style before he came, but after his arrival, there was more than a little. Churches "sprang up like mushrooms." In little more than a century (1066 to 1189), most of our beautiful Norman cathedrals were built. But, alas, few of these are in their original condition. Some are in ruins; others are fast crumbling away, while many have been rebuilt in parts in a later style or have been lost in alterations and improvements.

One of the oldest and most perfect examples of pure Norman may be seen in the beautiful chapel in the Tower of London (Plate XIX), and another in the Church of St. Bartholomew the Great, at Smithfield, near London.

Other examples are Durham Cathedral, Carlisle Cathedral, and the greater part of the Cathedrals of Peterborough and Rochester.

The family features of this style are very marked. You could recognise a member anywhere by its:

1. Thick walls,
2. Small windows,
3. Much decoration,
4. Deeply-recessed doors,
5. Huge piers and pillars,
6. And everywhere — the
   ROUND ARCH.

Sometimes the walls are covered with what Chaucer calls "hackings in masonry," the commonest "hacking" being a sculptured ornament in the shape of a diamond or lozenge, such as we saw in the Romanesque. But the favourite method of decorating wall surfaces remained, as in the latter style, the Arcade. These arcades are everywhere. They cover the walls, inside and outside; they adorn the front of the building; they even clamber up the tower: blind arcades, narrow interlacing arcades, and tiny arcades just under the eaves where the rooks build their nests—and sometimes all three kinds at once, in tiers one above the other.

NORMAN AND ROMANESQUE COMPARED

Our Norman cathedrals are not quite like their Romanesque cousins on the Continent.

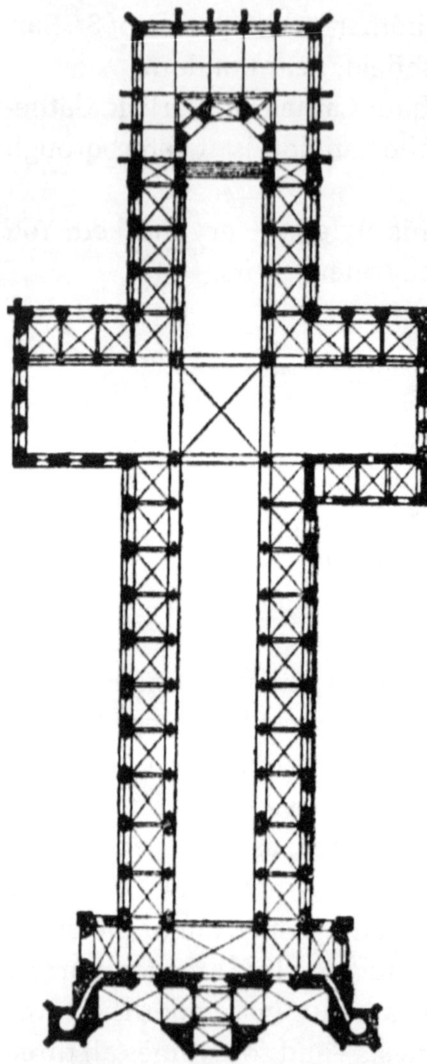

FIG. 45. - PETERBOROUGH CATHEDRAL PLAN

1. They are longer and narrower.

2. The roof is lower.

3. The arms of the cross extend farther.

4. In late Norman, there is frequently no apse at the east end.

These are the chief differences, and you will see them well illustrated if you compare the ground plan of Peterborough Cathedral in England (Fig. 45) with that of Pisa (Fig. 33), which, however, is somewhat exceptional because the arms of the cross extend unusually far.

A still better example would be Cologne Cathedral in Germany (Fig. 46) compared with our English Salisbury (Fig. 47), but these are not Romanesque. They belong to a later style — the Gothic.

It is quite natural that there should be these differences. If you were to take a little French or Italian boy out of his own country and bring him over to England to be educated, he would soon lose some of his French ways and become more like a little Briton. And

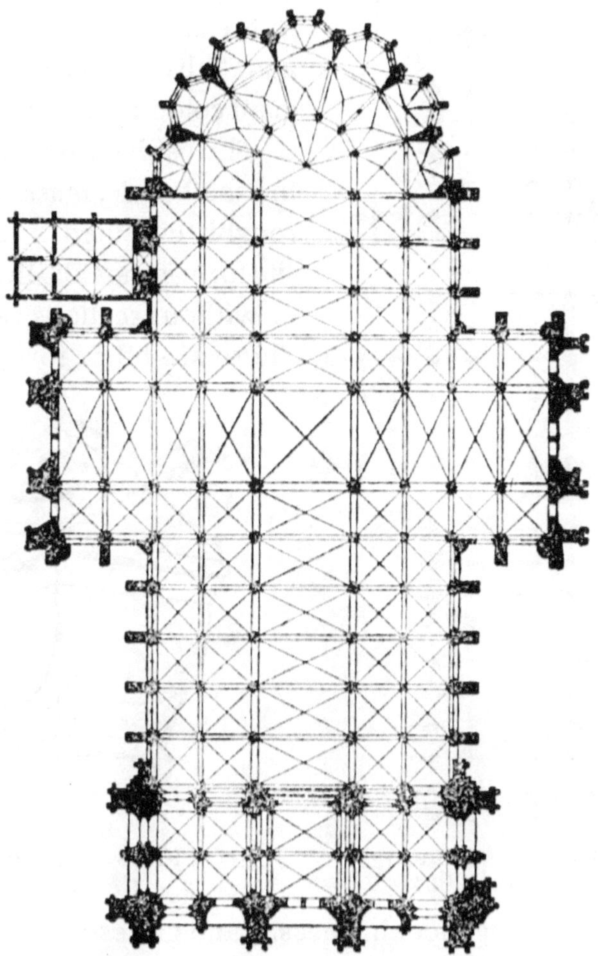

FIG. 46. - COLOGNE CATHEDRAL PLAN

so with this Romanesque style. When it was introduced into Britain, it adapted itself to its new surroundings — the climate, the material, the manners and customs, &c., of its adopted country — and began to assume a sturdy British look.

Among other changes, it became somewhat rougher, ruder, heavier. There is a church in England in which the pillars of the nave are almost as broad as they are long, and

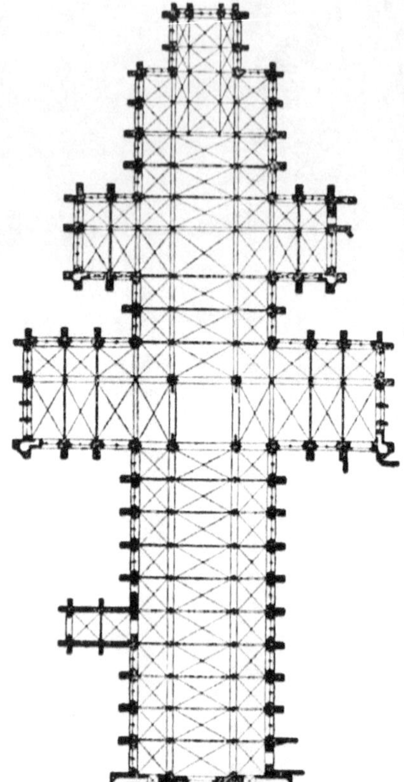

FIG. 47. -Salisbury
Cathedral Plan

in the cathedrals of Durham and Carlisle, you will see these giant columns in full strength.

The capitals are worthy of the shaft, rude, massive, often roughly executed. The favourite form is the CUSHION, with or without scallops (Fig. 48). There are other forms, such

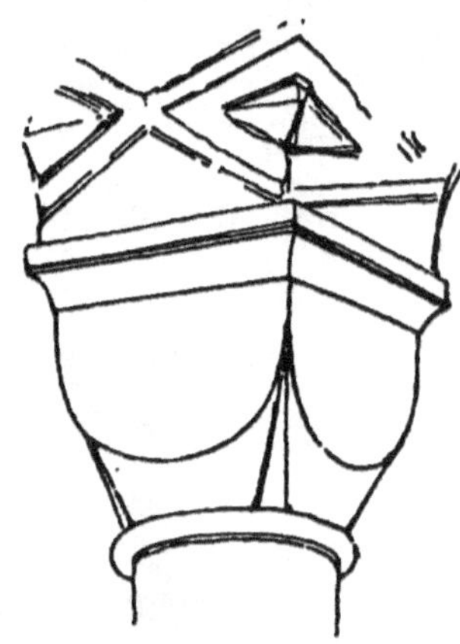

FIG. 48. - Cushion
Capital

as foliage, strange-looking beasts, and grotesque heads; but for one of these, you will meet with a dozen cushions.

Not very comfortable cushions, certainly! They would prove but a hard pillow for a weary head. And yet, they cannot be so hard as they look, or they would not crumble away as they do in the presence of their enemies — iron and lime. It is not the capitals alone that resent the intrusion of these, but every other part of the building. At the entrance of either iron or lime, the process of disintegration begins — a silent protest against their presence.

NORMAN WINDOWS

The most characteristic features in a Norman church, and the most decorated, are the doors and windows. At first, the windows are long, narrow, and single (Fig. 49); but as the style advanced, they increased in size and number.

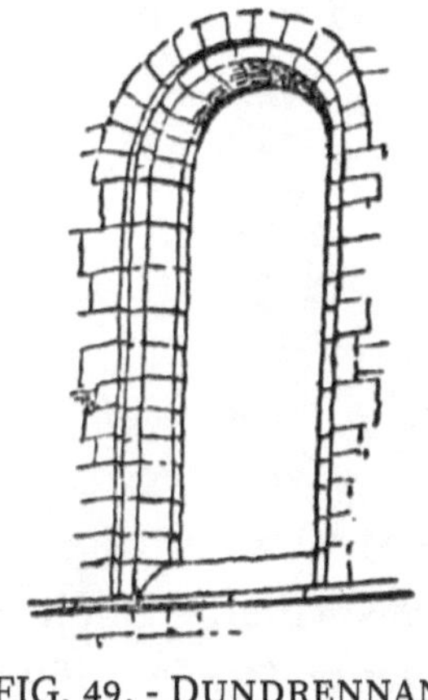

FIG. 49. - DUNDRENNAN ABBEY

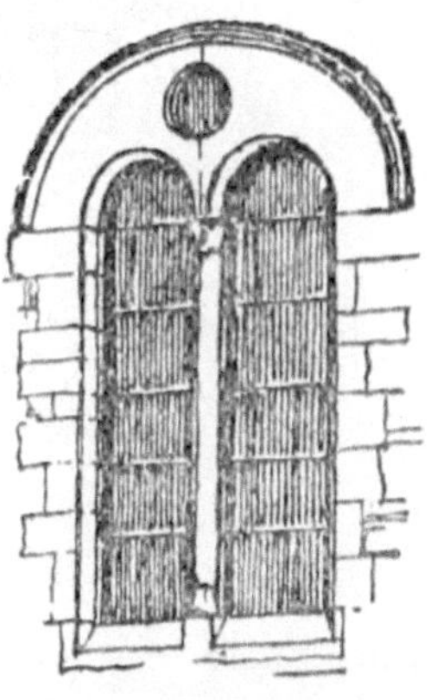

FIG 50. - S. MAURICE, YORK (GREEN BOND)

They began to be grouped in twos (Fig. 50). Sometimes, especially in belfries, two lights are divided by a shaft and included under one arch.

A still later form is the Triple Window with the biggest in the centre (Fig. 51).

Sometimes we find all these different kinds of windows in the same building: the single below, and the grouped ones above, in the triforium and clearstory.

The St. Catherine or Wheel Window is not so common as in

FIG. 51. - ROMSEY ABBEY (BOND.)

FIG. 52. - BURFRESTON CHURCH - EAST END

the Romanesque — at least not in early Norman — but here is a good example of one with eight well-defined spokes (Fig. 52).

A NORMAN DOORWAY

Even more striking than the windows are the Norman DOORWAYS. Fortunately for us, many of these beautiful doorways still remain when all the rest of the building has fallen into decay or been rebuilt in a later style. Sometimes, indeed, it is only by the doorway that you know you are looking at an old Norman building.

An interesting example is the Prior's Doorway in Ely Cathedral (Plate XX), the head of which is filled in solid with beautiful sculpture to the top of the arch. This doorway is rather exceptional, not in the extent of the decoration, but in its nature. As a rule, the latter consists of simple line patterns, just the zigzags, diamonds, lozenges, &c., that we saw

THE PRIOR'S DOORWAY, ELY CATHEDRAL
(SEE P. 80)

in the Romanesque. Taken singly, there does not seem much in these patterns, but when massed together, the effect is both rich and striking.

But it is not the sculpture alone that gives character to these doorways. Much of the effect is due to their DEPTH and to the succession of pillars and arches, one behind the other, that are cut in the thickness of the wall. Some of these walls are eight feet deep (a Norman castle might have walls 25 feet deep!), and these deep doorways followed naturally from the thickness of the wall.

But beautiful as these Norman doorways are, they cannot compare for a moment with the grand and imposing portals of the French and German cathedrals. This is indeed one of the chief distinctions between the Norman and the Romanesque. The latter has its richest decoration on the outside, while our Norman builders wisely reserved theirs for the interior, in deference, no doubt, to a British climate, which will not allow itself to be left out of consideration — for cold, and "fierce, and fickle" is the North!

And the same is true of the Gothic. Compare our Gothic façades with the magnificent façades of Amiens (see Frontispiece) and Chartres in France, or Cologne in Germany, or Milan in Italy. Still, every rule has its exceptions, and glorious ones too, for there is Durham Cathedral, and Peterborough Cathedral (Gothic), and Wells, and Ely — a mass of beautiful sculpture; and Iffley Church, Oxford, which is far from having a simple exterior. The walls are covered with patterns and decorated with interlacing arcades, and the plain cushion capitals of the Norman pillar have given place to more elaborate ones: then there is a Wheel Window, and, here and there, a POINTED ARCH!

What does it all mean? Simply this: that the Norman

is feeling its way to a new style, and we shall soon have to say good-bye to it. It has reached the Transition stage. Nothing is fixed. The walls are gradually getting thinner, the columns longer and slenderer, the roofs steeper, and the carving more delicate; and, in short, the solid, sturdy Norman, with its battlements and towers, is giving place to the graceful Gothic.

But before we say good-bye to it, we must have a look at a Norman Castle and a Scottish Abbey.

A NORMAN CASTLE

"In massive strength the castle frowned!" says Walter Scott, and this chapter will help you to understand this great writer when he is talking about a Norman castle.

Do you know the origin of these castles? When the Normans conquered England in 1066, they discovered that a conquered nation is an angry nation and a dangerous one, so they built these feudal castles all over the country for defense as well as for shelter.

Of course, the main thing wanted was strength.

They must withstand the foe: and so the site was all-important. Accordingly, we find them in the most extraordinary places — perched on the brow of a hill, or on an island in the center of a lake, or on the edge of a precipice, overhanging a steep cliff, and looking every moment as if it would topple down on the unfortunate passers-by below.

These castles are "like their work," as the Scotch say. Their decoration is of the useful order. We cannot expect to find architectural refinement and classical ornaments on them. Doric flutings and Corinthian capitals would not appeal very strongly to men who:—

"Carved at the meal with gloves of steel,
    And drank the red wine through the helmet barr'd."

No, their ornaments are of the sterner sort — battlements and towers and such like give variety of outline.

Suppose we examine one of these Norman castles (Plate XXI).

That great big square Tower in the center, with battlements and turrets and tiny slits for windows, is called the "Donjon" or "Keep."

It is the strongest part of the whole building. Here the Baron himself lived with his guests and retainers, feasting in the great banqueting hall, while his prisoners pined in the dungeons below.

A little difference, you see, between a Donjon and a Dungeon!

The open space or court round the tower was called a Bayley. Round the bayley was a high wall (the Barbican), surmounted by battlements and turrets, from which to defend the gate and the drawbridge. Those little round holes in the wall are not there for ornament, but for the defenders to pour out their arrows and stones on the besiegers.

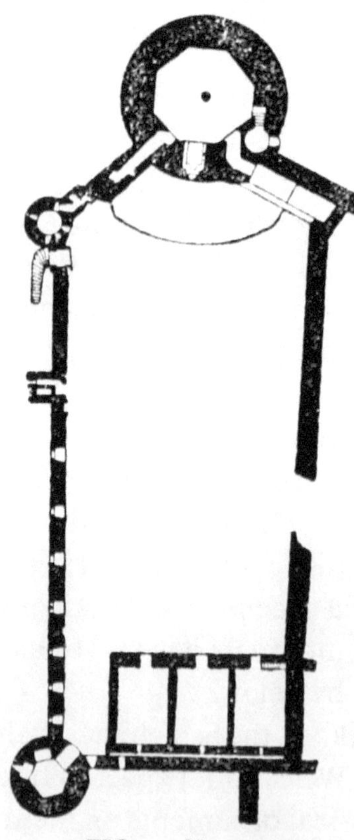

FIG. 53. NORMAN CASTLE BOTHWELL. (MACGIBBON & ROSS)

Round the whole site of the castle was a deep, broad ditch,

CARNARVON CASTLE, WALES
(SEE P. 84)

CAERLAVEROCK CASTLE, SCOTLAND

(SEE P. 87)

which could only be crossed by a drawbridge (see Plate XXII). An enemy does not seem to have had much chance with these Normans.

Remains of these old Norman castles are still to be seen at Rochester, Tunbridge, Bothwell, Conisburgh, Richmond in Yorkshire, Windsor, and the Tower of London (Fig. 53).

THE SCOTTISH BARONIAL

Well, these days of "feudal jars" are happily long since passed. Saxon and Norman have joined hands and become one nation. But occasionally we are reminded, in not unpleasant fashion, that such things were when, for example, in our wanderings in Bonnie Scotland, we come upon a peaceful mansion of recent date in which some of the features of these feudal times are retained for the sake of the picturesque effect.

Here, for instance, is Skibo Castle, Sutherlandshire (Plate XXIII), the home of the most peace-loving couple in the world; yet it bristles with battlements and loopholes and towers; and if you were to ask the fair owner why those symbols of horrid war in the sweet piping times of peace, she would look at you in mild surprise, and, with eyes fixed lovingly on the frowning towers, murmur:

"Oh, don't you like them? I think them just sweet!"

SOME SCOTTISH ABBEYS

The twelfth century was the great building century. David I, who was King of Scotland during part of this period, founded so many churches and abbeys that the Scots, who are very devout, made a saint of him. Another king, who reigned long after, and was much embarrassed for want of money, used to say sadly that David was "a sore saint for the crown."

Well, the sore saint might have spent his money in worse ways. For what would we have done without our beautiful abbeys? And what would Walter Scott have done? Some of his stories could not have been written. Then what could the artists have done who go North every year to draw these abbeys, and the French, and Germans, and Americans who come over to admire them? And what would the people themselves have done, who had no schools nor hospitals, and were taught and nursed in these abbeys? Yes, I think we must forgive David his extravagance.

Many of these beautiful abbeys are still standing — more or less in ruins.

There is Dunfermline Abbey — which was built by King David's father, Malcolm Canmore; and Kelso Abbey, and the beautiful abbey of Jedburgh (Plate XXIV), which owes much of its charm to its picturesque situation.

Then, among cathedrals that are more or less Norman (and, alas, more or less in ruins!), there is St. Magnus in Kirkwall, Leuchars Church in Fife, near St. Andrews, and the quaintly interesting Norman Church at Dalmeny. St. Magnus, Kirkwall, heads the list in a double sense, for it is the very earliest cathedral in Scotland, and also the farthest North—too far for many to see it. It has another distinction which it shares with one other (Glasgow Cathedral), namely that it is in entire preservation.

I daresay you are wondering why I do not mention Melrose Abbey, the most beautiful of them all, and the scene of part of Walter Scott's poem — "The Lay of the Last Minstrel," and Dryburgh Abbey, where the poet is buried; but these two are not Norman at all, but Gothic. There are other Scottish

SKIBO CASTLE, SUTHERLANDSHIRE
(*See p. 87*)

Photo, Graeme Smith

JEDBURGH ABBEY SCOTLAND
(SEE P. 96)

Abbeys that are partly Norman, and partly Gothic, and you will find it intensely interesting trying to discover for yourself which parts are Norman and which Gothic. You ought to be able to recognize the Norman at a glance, and when you have read the next chapter, you will, I hope, be equally familiar with the Gothic.

CHAPTER VI

GOTHIC ARCHITECTURE

THE POINTED ARCH

IF I were suddenly asked, "How would you know a Gothic building? Explain in one minute!" I should probably gasp out:

"By its: 1. Pointed Arch.

    2. Clustered Columns,

    3. Traceried Windows,

    4. Stained Glass,

    5. Vaulted Roof,

    6. Flying Buttress,

    7. Spires and Pinnacles,

    8. Gargoyles,

And — and — and —"

"Stop! Time's up!"

Ah, and there is so much more I had wanted to say. Still, it is a pretty good list and will help us to recognise a Gothic building when we see one. Not that every Gothic building has all these things, but most of them have some, and a few have all. They have many other things besides these — not "things" exactly, but mental qualities, for this Gothic is a very complex style, full of character.

In a list like this, it is difficult to say what should come first, but the Pointed Arch is, if anything, the most char-

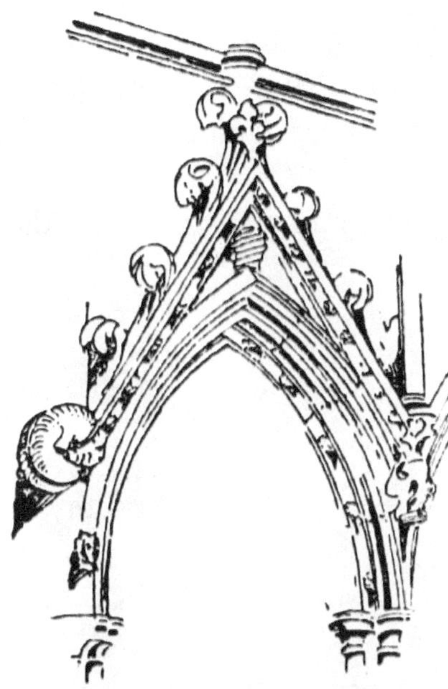

FIG. 54. - TOMB OF GILES DE BRIDFORD, SALISBURY CATHEDRAL. POINTED ARCH WITH GABLE AND CROCKETS.

acteristic feature. Indeed, we can scarcely think of the Gothic without it, though it is not an absolute test; there are many buildings with other forms. But the Gothic seems to delight in the pointed arch, and, to give it more point, she puts a Gable above it (Fig. 54 and Plate XXV and Frontispiece). Then she proceeds to adorn the sides of the gable with little curly ornaments, called "Crockets," or little crooks (Fig. 54), because they are supposed to resemble a shepherd's crook. That is, indeed, why they are there — as a symbol of the Good Shepherd, and a gentle reminder to the pastor of the church that he is the pastor or shepherd of his flock and will be expected to do the duties of a pastor.

There are many varieties of the Pointed Arch. One of the most graceful is the "Ogee" (Fig. 55). If you look carefully, you will observe that the Ogee has a double curve. The upper part is concave or hollow, and the lower half is convex or round.

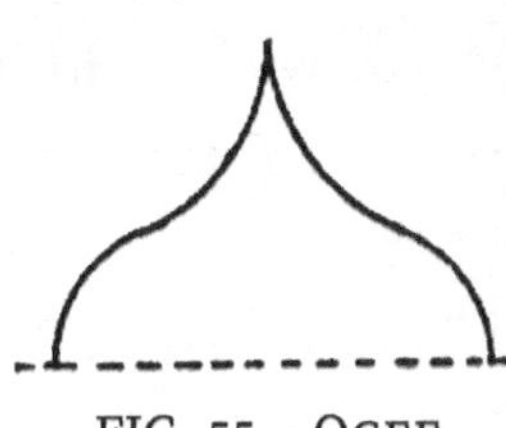

FIG. 55. - OGEE

Compare Fig. 55 with Figs. 57 and 58, and you will see the difference. The latter have one curve only, the convex.

Here is another Ogee arch, which has not only crockets and a gable, but is beautifully cusped (Fig. 56). The cusps are those fascinating little projecting points which separate the small arcs within the larger arch. There is nothing more decorative than cusps, and nothing more common, especially in Middle and Late Gothic.

The Arch, like everything else, had a History — a Rise,

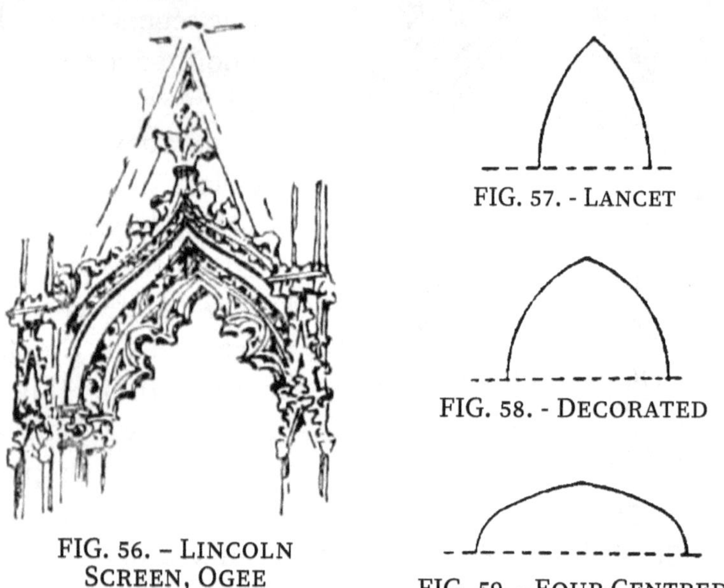

FIG. 56. – LINCOLN SCREEN, OGEE ARCH CUSPED

FIG. 57. - LANCET

FIG. 58. - DECORATED

FIG. 59. - FOUR CENTRED

Decline, and Fall. When it first appears, it is long and narrow, slender and graceful (Fig. 57). Then, in the Middle Ages, it sacrifices a little of its length in favour of breadth, but as it is always beautifully decorated at this stage, we do not miss the slenderness and grace (Fig. 58). In Old Age, you would hardly recognise it. It is just the ghost of its former self; for it has widened out and flattened down till it has lost all character and nearly all "point," and with its "point," its existence. For what is a Pointed Arch without a "point" (Fig. 59)?

ROUEN CATHEDRAL
(*See pp. 93, 123*)

THE CLUSTERED COLUMN

You remember the classical column standing apart from its fellows in dignified isolation. What a contrast this is to the Gothic, which is as sociable as it is graceful (Fig. 60). It

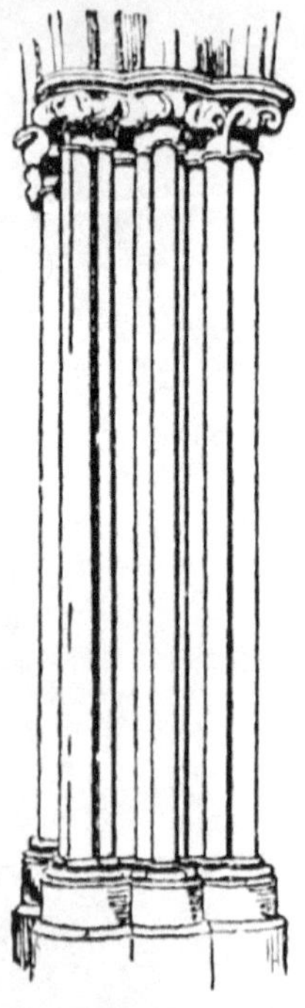

FIG. 60. - CLUSTERED COLUMN, WELLS

FIG. 61. - FOUR LITTLE SHAFTS ATTACHED TO CENTRE COLUMN, CHRISTCHURCH HANTS. (BOND.)

was not always so, however. The process by which the single shaft grew into the clustered column was a very gradual one. At first, four little shafts attached themselves to the central column. Then eight other smaller shafts joined on to the first four — in groups, one on each side. Then, by degrees, they drew still closer together — "fore-gathered," as the Scots say — till at last they completely encircled and hid the big central shaft (Figs. 60 and 61). Sometimes you will see them with their heads apart, while their bodies (or shafts) are locked together, as if they had protested against being merged altogether in the general mass, and hoped in this way to preserve their own identity, or some small fraction of it.

TRACERIED WINDOWS

Did you ever wonder how church windows came to be traceried — that is, cut into such beautiful and intricate forms and patterns? We do not have Traceried windows in our houses. We look through windows more or less square and plain and practical. It would be rather amusing, would it not, to look through a window shaped like a cloverleaf, or a shamrock, as in Fig. 62, or one with four leaves (Fig. 63), or five (Fig. 64)?

FIG. 62. - Trefoil   FIG. 63. - Quatrefoil   FIG. 64. - Cinquefoil

Such windows are said to be foliated (Latin "folium," or, if you prefer it, French "feuille," a leaf), and the number of leaves is expressed by a prefix. Thus a 3-leaved window is called a Trefoil window, a 4-leaved one a Quatrefoil, and a 5-leaved one a Cinquefoil.

You will see beautiful examples of all three in Figs. 65, 66, and 67; and not of these only, but also, associated with them, of sexfoils and multifoils, which mean six leaves and many leaves.

These are not the only kinds of traceried windows, nor

are they the earliest. The order of Tracery in point of time is as follows:

1. Plate Tracery (Fig. 50).
2. Geometrical Tracery (Figs. 65, 66, 67).
3. Flowing Tracery (Plate XXVI).
4. Perpendicular Tracery (Fig. 68, Plate XXIX).

In France and Germany, there is practically no Perpendicular, but a variant of the Flowing Tracery called Flamboyant, because of its supposed resemblance to flames (Frontispiece).

The first is the simplest; the second and third the most graceful; and the last the most practical.

But we have not seen yet how these Traceried Windows came to be there at all, for it was not a case of an architect waking up one fine morning and saying, "Lo! We shall have Traceried Windows!" The growth of Tracery had a more natural and reasonable origin. It was a direct result of the increasing size of the window in Gothic architecture. Long ago, in the early days of the Romanesque, when the windows were small and single, there was not much room for Tracery; but by and by, two lights appeared, then by degrees, one light after another linked itself on to the first, till there was a whole succession of lights — two, three, four, five, six, seven, eight, and even nine — all in a row, and forming one huge window! Over this was placed a great boundary arch; leaving between the tops of the lights and the top of the confining arch a triangular space, something like a shield in form. It was to fill this space (the Spandrel) that Window Tracery was invented.

At first, this was of the simplest order, just two or three circular holes, or penetrations, as they are called, pierced through the plate or slab of stone, and hence called Plate Tracery (see Fig. 50). But by and by, these circular openings

FIG. 65. - St Albans
Cathedral Trefoils

FIG. 66. - Westminster
Chapter House.
Quatrefoils and Sexfoil

were foliated — that is, cut into trefoils, quatrefoils, and cinquefoils, and other geometrical forms, as we have just seen. That is called Geometrical Tracery (Figs. 65, 66, 67).

The next step in the history of Tracery is a curious one. Up till now, the eye of the beholder had rested only on the holes or circular lights, not on the spaces that separated them. The form of the hole was everything, the form of the intervening

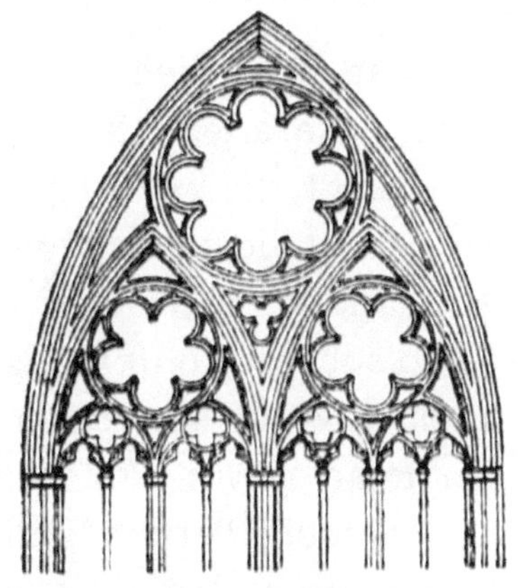

FIG. 67. - Binham.
Cinquefoil and
Multifoil

FIG. 68. - Ashby St
Ledger Panelled
Perpendicular. (Bond.)

stonework nothing. But as these holes grew bigger and bigger, and drew together closer and closer, the stonework spaces that separated them naturally grew smaller and smaller till at last they appeared as mere ribs or bars. And now, for the first time, they caught the eye of the beholder! And, as if conscious of having done so, and under a genial sense of their own growing importance, these bars of stone suddenly lost their stony nature, and became soft as wax; bending and twisting and writhing in every direction, and forming all sorts of intricate and elaborate figures! That is what is meant by Flowing Tracery, of which Plate XXVI is an example. Two other beautiful examples are the great west window in York Minster and the east window in Carlisle Cathedral.

PERPENDICULAR TRACERY (Fig. 68)

But these beautiful windows with the Flowing Tracery did not last very long.

"A rose's brief bright life of joy,
Such unto them was given."

Whether it was that, like the rose, they died of their own loveliness, or from some other cause, after a time they ceased to be. The graceful curves unbent, the bars of stone straightened themselves out again, and stood up stiff, erect, and rigid. Instead of beautiful and intricate forms delicate as lacework, there was to be seen a succession of straight lines, perpendicular and horizontal, crossing each other at right angles, and giving rise to the name by which this kind of tracery is everywhere known — namely, Perpendicular (Fig. 68 and Plate XXIX). But there is something to be said for these Perpendicular Windows — some people would say that there was a good deal to be said, for they give us light, more light than the fanciful ones do, and, after all, one of the chief duties of a window is supposed to be to give light.

STAINED WINDOWS

> "And storied windows, richly dight,
> Casting a dim religious light."

In Early English, the windows were narrow, admitting very little light; but, as the style advanced, the windows grew bigger, till, at last, the whole church was flooded with light. Not always white light. Sometimes the light shone through stained glass, and reflected all the colors of the rainbow. These beautiful stained windows were the glory of the Gothic cathedrals.

Good modern stained glass is done in exactly the same way as the old. That is to say, glass of different colors is taken and fitted together like a mosaic, and such things as the features of a face, hands, feet, etc., are painted in a clean, strong line on almost clear glass. The main thing to remember is that in stained glass the light shines through the picture, and in an oil painting the light shines on the picture. The quality that glass should have, therefore, is clearness. The color should be simple, and should glisten and scintillate like rubies and emeralds. A window is not intended to obscure the light, but to let the light through. It must also keep out the weather; consequently, the glass should be thick and strong, and the leads into which the different pieces of glass are fitted should also be thick and strong, or else, some windy night, the window will be blown in. Plates XXVII and XXVIII are interesting examples of modern stained glass.

But to return to our old Gothic windows. Sometimes they

tell a story — the story of "The Beautiful Life." The Angel appearing to Mary with the glad tidings that she was to be the mother of Our Savior, or the Shepherds tending their flocks by night, or the Wise Men following the Star in the East till it led them to a manger in Bethlehem. And very precious these "storied windows" must have been to the people in olden times, when books were dear, and few could afford them, or read them if they had them.

Another great advantage about these glass pictures was that they were always there! They did not get torn, like the pictures in story books; or fade away, like those on canvas; or melt away, like the pictures painted by the sun. What, you've never seen the sun's pictures? Then you must have been asleep, for he paints the skies every morning and every evening. (It is a pity that he wipes out his pictures almost as soon as he has painted them in.) He does his best work before breakfast and after supper, when bidding the world "Good-night." I caught him at work one morning very, very early, before anybody was up, except the blackbirds and the finches. There he was behind a belt of trees, painting the sky in all the colors of the rainbow, and converting the forest into one vast cathedral. Tiny patches of sapphire and crimson and gold gleamed like mosaics in between the pine branches; only the colors were not fixed, as in the cathedral window, but kept on always changing, like the figures in a kaleidoscope. And how the blackbirds and finches were enjoying it all! It was a full choral service that morning. With what glee they sang their morning hymn:

"This is the day which the Lord hath made,
Let us rejoice and be glad therein!"
Chirp! Chirp!

Their joy seemed to inspire the sun, for all at once he

YORK MINISTER
(*See pp. 98, 102*)

came out from behind the belt of trees and looked round him with a broad smile, and, as he did so, all the hills burst into flame and burned like opals!

Then I knew where the inventor of stained windows got his inspiration.

THE VAULTED ROOF

"The spacious firmament on high,
With all the blue ethereal sky,
And spangled heavens, a shining frame,
Their great Original proclaim." — ADDISON.

That is what they were singing in the cathedral (see Plate XXIX), and, as they sang, they were thinking of the vault of heaven with its real stars, not of any vault above their head with its stars of stone. But it is the stone stars that we are concerned with. How came they to be there? Well, it is rather a long story, and to understand it, we must go back to the days of the old Romans.

You remember their vault; a simple semi-circular structure like a tunnel — about the simplest form possible (Fig. 69). But how proud the Romans were of it! It was the joy of their heart. You see, it was their own invention (or very nearly so), and, as Shakespeare says, "an ill-favoured thing, but mine own"; which

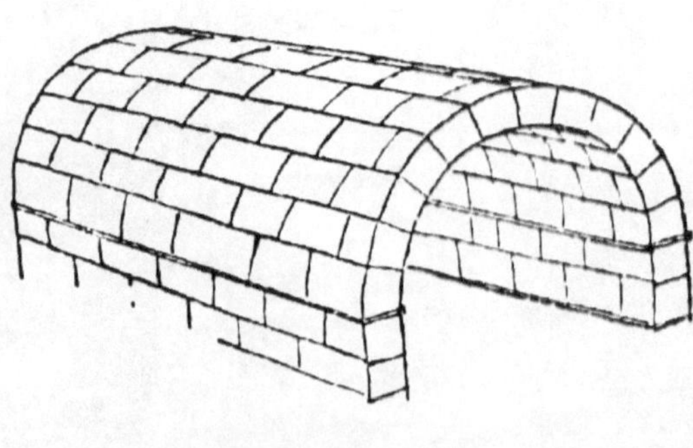

FIG. 69. - ROMAN BARREL VAULT

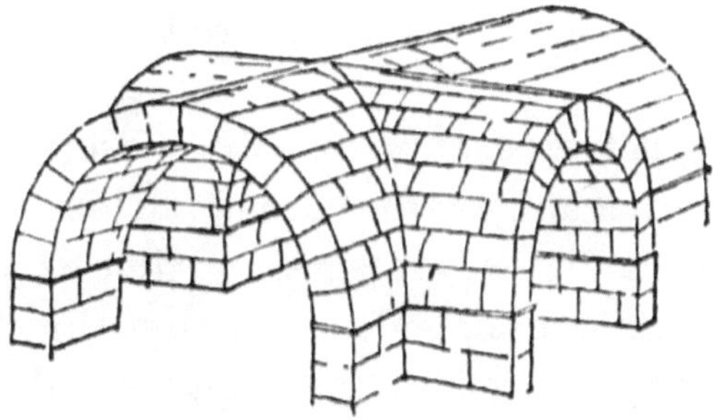

FIG. 70. - Intersecting Groined Vault

just means that what belongs to oneself has a very special charm for oneself.

You notice I said "very nearly so." Strictly speaking, it was not quite their own invention, for the Romans had got their idea of the vault from their neighbors, the Etruscans, who had used it in the construction of their Cloaca Maxima, or great drain. But if the Etruscans were the actual inventors, the Romans were the first to make extensive practical use of this vault. They were quick enough to see all its possibilities, and they delighted in it and used it on all occasions — for their temples and theatres, and palaces, and public baths, and everywhere.

But after a time, the Romans discovered that there is nothing perfect on earth, not even a Barrel Vault, and accordingly, they set to work to invent a new kind of Vault that would have all the virtues of the first and none of its little weaknesses. The result was ingenious. Perhaps on the principle that two heads are better than one, they put Barrel Vault number two through Barrel Vault number one, cutting away the corners, and thus producing a kind of double Barrel Vault. This is known as the Intersecting Bar-

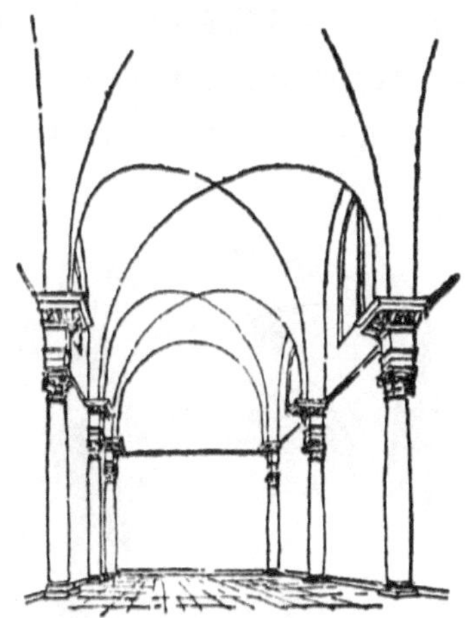

FIG. 71. - Intersecting Groined Vault

rel Vault, or, still better, as the Intersecting Groined Vault (Figs. 70 and 71).

The new vault gave great satisfaction for a time. It served its purpose; it was fire-proof and weather-proof; but (why is there always a "but"?) with all its advantages, and they were many, it had one or two little disadvantages. For one thing, it was clumsy, very clumsy, especially where spaces of different sizes had to be roofed. So once more, these master-builders put their heads together to invent something that would be graceful as well as strong, and after years and years of thinking and planning, they at last found a solution to the difficulty. You will smile when you hear what it was — it all seems so simple.

They added a Point to the Arch!

"What!" you say, "just a little point?"

Yes, but that "little point" made all the difference.

The two arches now intersected beautifully.

The next step was to strengthen the vault still further by putting "RIBS" over the parts where one arch goes through (or crosses) the other, with an ornament, called a Boss, at the point of intersection. These "Ribs" were found to be so useful, and at the same time so decorative, that in time more

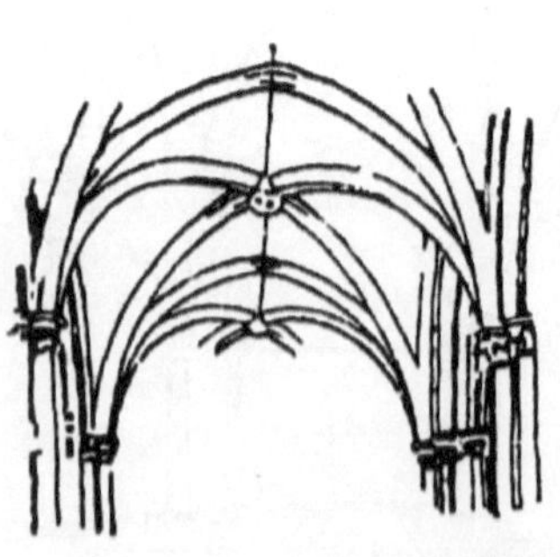

FIG. 72. - PLAIN
QUADRIPARTITE VAULT

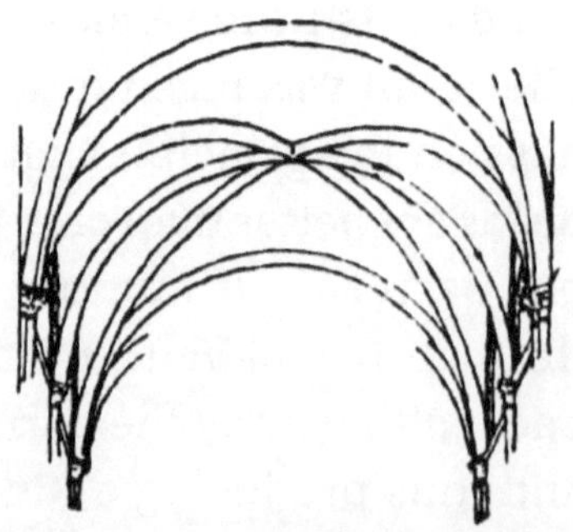

FIG. 73. - SEXPARTITE
VAULT

were added in different directions, some of them beautifully moulded; till, at last, the whole vaulted roof was covered with a grand network of interlinking "Ribs" and "Bosses."

That is what is meant by RIB VAULTING.

But where are our stars?

They have not come out yet: we need some more "Ribs."

You remember how we began with two, crossing diagonally, so (Fig. 72).

Suppose we put another "Rib" through the first two, from side to side, making six triangular spaces or compartments (Fig. 73).

Now, is there room for any more ribs?

Yes! We might put in some short ones between the long ones; they will not carry much, but they will look effective (Fig. 74).

Now, that is just what the Gothic builders did. They put in a short rib between each of these six spokes, and out came — a Star — not one, but many, a whole galaxy of them (Fig. 75). And those stars will never set like the real ones. They will not hide themselves on a cloudy night, or a rainy one, but will look down on us with as kindly a smile on a fair summer

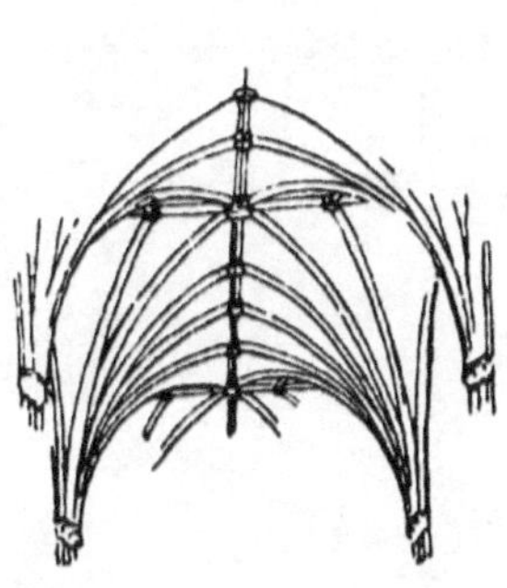

FIG. 74. - TIERCERON VAULT WITH RIDGES

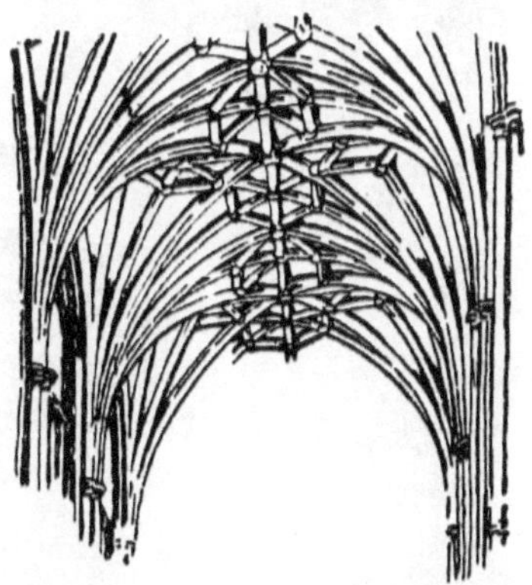

FIG. 75. CANTERBURY NAVE. (LIERNE) VAULT OF STAR TYPE

MELROSE, ABBEY
(SEE P. 109)

"WHERE BUTTRESS ALTERNATIVELY SEEM FRAMED OF EBON AND IVORY."

evening as on a dark winter one, quite unconcerned whether it be June or December, Midsummer Day or New Year's Eve.

But hark! What is that they are singing in the cathedral?

> "What though in solemn silence all
> Move round the dark terrestrial ball?
> What though no real voice, nor sound
> Amidst their radiant orbs be found?
>
> In Reason's ear they all rejoice,
> And utter forth a glorious voice,
> For ever singing as they shine,
> The hand that made us is divine."

"Divine?" Yes! And the hands that made these cathedral stars, the hands that fashioned with such loving care those stars of stone, and put them there in the vaulted roof for our delight, are not they too, in their own way, "divine"?

BUTTRESS AND FLYING BUTTRESS

Plate XXX is a picture of Melrose Abbey.

You see those great grey blocks, standing like sentinels round the building. These are the "Buttresses," and it is their duty to "buttress" or "bolster up" the Main Wall, which has a tendency to fall outwards with the weight of the roof (Figs. 76 and 77).

Now I think you will agree with me that these Buttresses serve a very useful purpose: for as "Alice in Wonderland" says - "One of the most serious things that can possibly happen to one is to get one's head cut off": and we might add, as a very good second, "to have one's sides cave in, or burst out!"

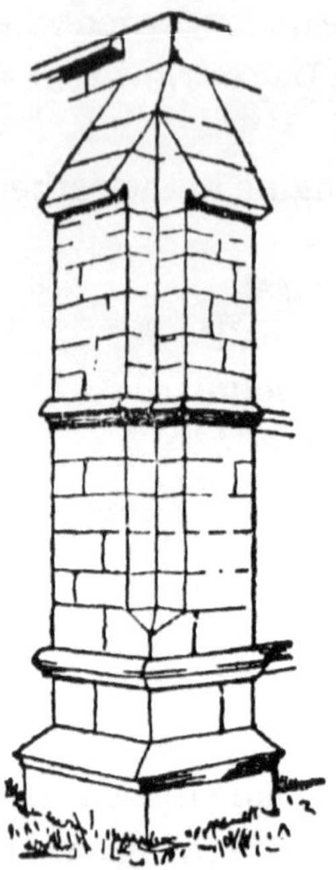

FIG. 76. - EARLY
ENGLISH BUTTRESS

FIG. 77. - PERPENDICULAR
BUTTRESS

But the Buttresses are not alone in their good work. Sometimes they are helped by the "Flying Buttresses," those graceful arches that go from the big main or Mother Wall to the little wall of the aisles (Fig. 78).

Here they come, all in a row, like a flight of swallows (Plate XXX). And what a little "fly" it is after all! Just enough to show them how it is done, and what a delightful thing it is, and then say "Goodbye" to such joys for ever. For, scarcely have they started, when they come bump up against these stern sentinels that keep watch and ward over the whole: not another inch do they get: that is their first and only flight.

Ah, but they are glad to be there too — glad and proud — for they know that they are helping to support "Mother Wall," and keep her from coming to grief; and they feel very important with their little backs up against her big back. "Here we are, Mother! holding you up: so don't be afraid if you should feel like breaking down, or coming to bits, or rather top-heavy, or your head flying off — or anything else unpleasant. We're here!"

FIG. 78. - FLYING BUTTRESS, CHRISTCHURCH, HANTS. (ARCH. ASSO. SKETCH)

Sometimes the little birds alight on them, and tell each other stories of what they have seen in their flight. Then the "Flying Buttresses" listen and grow restless — wings at their shoulders seem to play — and they feel as if they would give anything in the world for another little flight; but they only hold on all the faster. For they know that they are the precious link that binds all together — that, if they were to desert, all might fall apart in hopeless confusion and, rather than that, they will stand there bolstering up Mother Wall to the end of their days.

SPIRES AND PINNACLES

Gothic Cathedrals, especially the early ones, are usually crowned with a spire.

A Spire is just an elongated pyramid; that is, one that has been stretched up and up and up till it reaches far into the sky. The highest spire in all England, and the most beautiful, belongs to Salisbury Cathedral (Plate XXXIII).

There are great varieties of spires. Some are shaped like a sugar loaf — conical. Some have eight sides — that is a very common kind in England — and here is a spire, St. Michael's Coventry, supported by eight flying buttresses (Fig. 79).

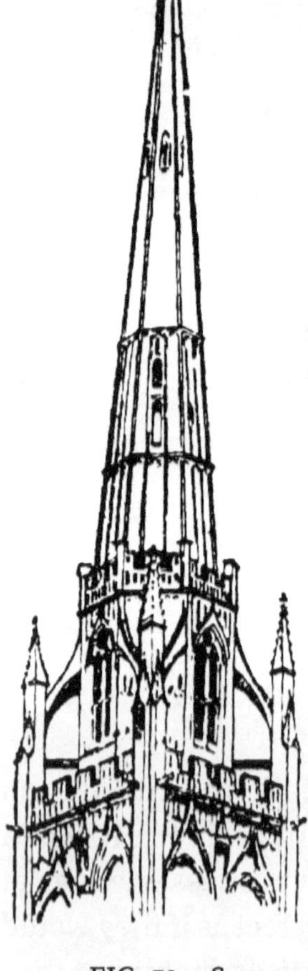

FIG. 79. - S. MICHAEL'S.

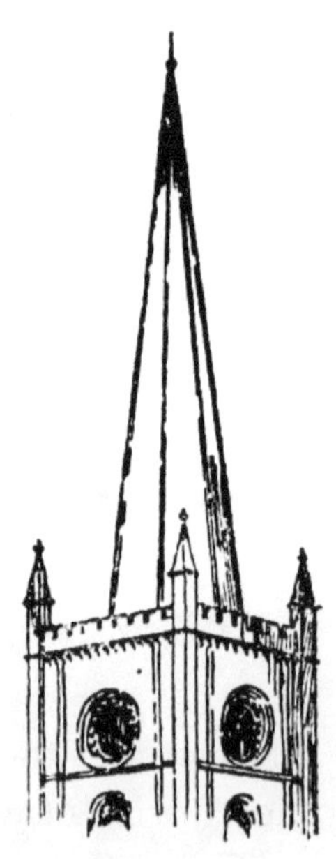

FIG. 80. - STRATFORD ON AVON SPIRE

You will like this spire because it belongs to Shakespeare's birthplace, Stratford-on-Avon (Fig. 80). Those four

GARGOYLES, NOTRE DAME, PARIS
(SEE P. 115)

GARGOYLE, NOTRE DAME, PARIS
(*See p. 115*)

little things at the corner are baby spires or Pinnacles. They all hope to be real spires some day, but they never will. They will just be pinnacles to the end of their days.

GARGOYLES

You remember those funny Grotesques we saw on the Romanesque cathedral? Well, here is something almost as funny on a Gothic cathedral. Those queer-looking creatures are just the carved ends of water-spouts, and they are called "Gargoyles" or "Gurgoyles," because of the gurgling noise that the water makes when passing through them (Plates XXXI and XXXII).

You will notice a rather wicked expression on the face of some of these Gargoyles. That is because they are supposed to represent the evil spirits or little imps escaping from the church. For the same reason, they generally take the form of uncanny creatures — griffins, dragons, and such like, animals with a slightly bad reputation.

That is the usual explanation, but one learned writer, a bishop, suggests a much happier one. After describing some extraordinary Gargoyles in a French church, he says they seem to him like an appeal to all creatures to praise the Lord — "dragons and all deeps, beasts and all cattle, creeping things and flying fowl."

Whether true or not, this is a beautiful idea, and we would like to believe it!

"THE THREE GOTHICS"

"Early English," or Thirteenth-Century Gothic"

FIG, 81. - EARLY ENGLISH
DOGTOOTH ORNAMENT

FIG. 82. - EARLY ENGLISH CAPITAL
(PRIOR.) LINCOLN TRANSEPT

"Well, really," I can hear you say, "this Gothic is very puzzling. Last year I saw Salisbury Cathedral (Plate XXXIII), and was told that it was 'Gothic,' and this summer I saw Roslin Chapel, near Edinburgh, and next day King's College Chapel, Cambridge, and again the guide said 'Gothic' — But how can that be? How can three buildings so very unlike belong to the same style?"

But they do! Only the one is thirteenth-century Gothic, and the others fourteenth and fifteenth-century Gothic, and the difference between these three is as great as the difference between a little girl of thirteen, and the same girl at fourteen and fifteen.

At thirteen she (the Gothic) is all simplicity, and good taste, and quiet manners; very correct and decorous, and what is called "conventional," that is, liking to be and do like everybody else.

Her favourite ornament is the "Dogtooth" (Fig. 81) and her Capitals are adorned with a wreath of rather prim leaves, with stiff

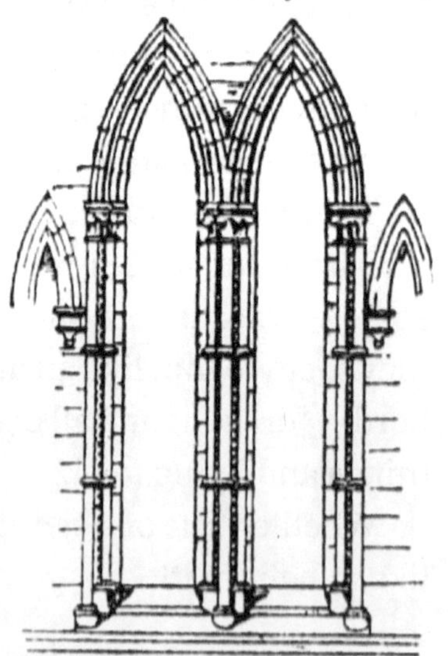

FIG. 83. -EARLY ENGLISH
LANCET WINDOW.
LINCOLN CATHEDRAL,
C. 1220. (PARKER.)

SALINSBURY CATHEDRAL
(*See* pp. *116, 124*)

stems (Fig. 82). Her windows are the simple Lancet (Fig. 83). Certainly, she does not err on the side of over-decoration. "Nothing too much" seems to be her motto.

"DECORATED," OR FOURTEENTH-CENTURY GOTHIC

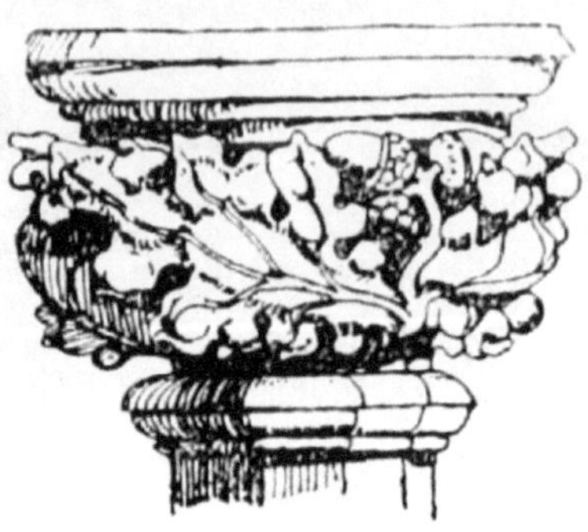

FIG. 84. - ELY CATHEDRAL

At fourteen the Gothic takes much more pride in her appearance, and adorns herself profusely (see Plate XXXIV), but always with exquisite taste, for her ornament is not only beautiful in itself, but also well placed. She seems to say — "Oh, what a beautiful world this is! How I love its trees and its streams! I am going to make

FIG. 85. - SOUTHWELL CATHEDRAL.
MEDIXEAL FOLIAGE. (COLLINS)

myself a wreath of oak (Fig. 84) and one of maple, and one of vine-leaves, and wear them joyfully (Fig. 85). And I shall put a little round ball into every hollow and cranny I can find, to remind me of the beautiful buds in my garden (Fig. 86). And I shall place a Rose window like a star in the centre of my forehead, behind which the sun will set in flames of crimson and gold, and the moon rise, cold and fair, to light the weary traveller on his way."

FIG. 86. - DECORATED BALL
FLOWER ORNAMENT

"PERPENDICULAR," OR LATE GOTHIC

But by the time the Gothic reaches her fifteenth year, her taste changes. She grows dull and rigid, and delights in quite other ornaments. Instead of a bud, she puts a full-blown flower into her crannies and hollows (Fig. 87), the stiffest flower you ever saw, enclosed in four straight lines, forming a square: and, instead of oak leaves and the ivy and the vine, she adorns her-

FIG. 87. - TUDOR CRESTING. HENRY
VII CHAPEL, WESTMINSTER

self with shields and crests — things which show the pride of Man, not the joy of Nature.

Here, for instance, is a building covered all over with arms and crests, and mottoes, as if the owner were shouting at us all the way down:

> "I am the crest of Sir Leoline Tall,
> And I cover the windows and ceilings and all!"

We feel inclined to say, with Humpty Dumpty in the story book:

> "All right! but I wish you would not shout so loud."

Another thing that this fifteenth-century Gothic delights in is straight up-and-down lines, crossed with horizontal lines. She puts them everywhere: on walls, and windows, and doors, and screens, and even on columns. This sort of decoration is called Panelling. (Plate XXXV.)

The people who admire this style like to visit a certain chapel in Westminster Abbey, built by Henry VII for himself, where they get enough straight lines to last them many a long day. And not straight lines only! For, when they have done admiring the walls, they turn their eyes up to the ceiling, and there they see what looks like a Forest of Fans, so graceful and fairylike that they wonder if they can have strayed into a wood by mistake. (Plate XXXVI.)

So you see the "Perpendicular" is not always stiff and rigid. She can unbend when she likes, and when she does unbend, she is delightful. Like the little girl in the nursery rhyme who, when she was good, was very VERY good, but when she was bad, she was horrid.

If you want to know just how good the "Perpendicular" can be, you must go to her beloved Oxford and Cambridge, where she bestows her brightest smiles; and if you don't come back fascinated, I give you up.

"What about the straight lines?"

Oh, they are there, of course, but so cunningly overlaid with exquisite ornament, that we almost forget that they are straight, and certainly should never dream of calling them "stiff" or "rigid."

Indeed, we wonder how we could have applied such uncomplimentary adjectives to a style so rich, so dainty, so decorative, so altogether delightful as the Perpendicular.

GOTHIC SYMBOLISM AND MYSTERY

I once asked a lover of animals and of architecture what she considered the highest virtue in the latter.

"Adaptability!" was the reply. "The noblest architecture is full of adaptation, not of one style to another, nor of one nationality to another, but of all means to the desired end."

Judged by this standard, the Gothic must take a high place. Now, adaptability does not mean weakness. Strong characters are often the most adaptable, and our Gothic is adaptable from strength, not weakness.

It has some very decided articles of faith, but it does not insist on these at all times and seasons, and on all occasions. It loves the Pointed Arch, for instance, but, where this form is inconvenient, it freely adopts the Round Arch. It believes in sloping roofs; and in cold northern climes, where these are almost a necessity to get rid of the snow and rain as quickly as possible, it usually makes the slope very great; while in warm, dry climates, like Italy, where there is no such necessity, it contents itself with a moderate slope. But you must not suppose from this that the Gothic is wanting in character.

TOMB OF MARY QUEEN OF SCOTS, WESTMINSTER ABBEY
(SEE P. 120)

Quite the contrary. It has as much character as a Scottish climate. It is never dull, or flat or stupid, or uninteresting. It loves laughter. It loves variety and odd numbers, threes, and fives and sevens. It loves odd sizes. If it has three towers, one of them will be bigger than the other two. (See Amiens Cathedral, Frontispiece.) If it has five windows, they will often be of different sizes and different forms, with different patterns and traceries. It loves Symbolism!

Everything about a Gothic cathedral is symbolic. Its general form, a Latin Cross, still further emphasized by the cross that crowns its gable — the tall spire, pointing ever heavenward; and the crockets that creep and climb up its sides, symbolic of the office of shepherd.

And lastly, much of the fascination of the Gothic lies in its sense of Mystery. This quality always appeals to us. We like a story with a mystery, and we are interested in a character that we do not wholly understand — one that leaves something to the imagination, something to be found out.

Now, there is no mystery about the Greek Temple. It is very beautiful and very definite — stately, serene, and simple. We can take it all in at once: we can count its columns, number its flutings, and see all round them.

But not so the Gothic Cathedral. We cannot grasp it all at once; we cannot exhaust it after many months: it is full of Mystery.

"We gaze untired into the dimness of the lofty roof, we mark the height, the space, the gloom, the glory — a burst of sunlight kindles 'the giant windows' blazoned fires'; a passing cloud darkens the vaulted aisles with awe-inspiring shadows, and in the delicate traceries and fantastic carvings we find food for continual delight."

When we stand before the cathedrals of Chartres or Rouen (Plate XXV), or Amiens (Frontispiece), or our own familiar Salisbury (Plate XXXIII), we feel that the builders of them were inspired by a profound religious enthusiasm.

> "They builded better than they knew,
> The conscious stone to beauty grew."

And to enjoy them we must try to catch something of their spirit. There is a story told of the artist, John Opie. A gentleman seeing him at work, and anxious to discover the secret of his success, inquired eagerly: "What do you mix your colours with, Mr. Opie?"

"With brains, sir!" was the reply.

Now we must mix our knowledge not only with brains but with sympathy if we want these cathedrals to speak to us; if they are to be more to us than just so many buildings of a certain form, with vaulted roof and painted windows and all the rest of it.

> "For out of Thought's interior sphere,
> These wonders rose to upper air";

and we want to catch the thought, to feel the mystery, and to enter into the joy of the builders.

CHAPTER VII

RENAISSANCE ARCHITECTURE

THE AWAKENING

NO! This is not a prison you are looking at (Plate XXXVII), but a palace! A palace of the Grand Style,

the Italian Style,

the Florentine Style,

the roomy, gloomy, spacious, severe, symmetrical

Renaissance Style.

Here are all our old Roman "orders" once more, and Roman arches, and Roman ornaments.

What does it mean? Have we fallen asleep like Rip Van Winkle, and are we still dreaming — dreaming of Old Rome and the palace of the Caesars?

No! It is not we who have fallen asleep, but Europe that has wakened up — wakened to discover that she possesses untold treasures in the old classic writers, and the monuments they describe. People of all nations are looking back lovingly to the good old times, as we shall never cease to call the Past, and are trying to bring them back.

They are studying Vitruvius and other old Roman writers on architecture with an eagerness that amounts almost to a passion: they are measuring old Roman monuments, and raising new ones modelled on these. Not all alike. This one, the Strozzi Palace (Plate XXXVII), belongs to Florence, and is rather heavy and stern. There are much more cheerful ones in Venice and Rome, and in some countries these new buildings are more than cheerful — they are positively gay.

A number of causes have contributed to this awakening, this Re-birth or Renaissance, as it is called — of which the two foremost are the invention of printing, and the taking of Constantinople by the Turks. It seems strange how that could have had such an effect; but when Constantinople fell into the hands of the Turks, the Greek and Latin scholars who were congregated there fled with their precious manuscripts, and spread them- selves and their learning all over Europe. The grand old classics, which had been shut up for centuries in libraries to which only the few had access, were translated into other languages, and everyone was eagerly drinking in the new knowledge.

So much for the causes of this awakening. Let us look at the results — as they affected Architecture.

The Renaissance was a new thing. Now a new thing is not always or necessarily a good thing, and in this case the good-ness was only relative.

"Have you been a good boy to-day?" asked a fond father of his son.

"Fairly so, father!" was the conscientious reply.

I am afraid this Renaissance style was only "fairly so."

"What would constitute goodness in an architecture you ask?

Well, that depends. Some people would say "purity," oth-ers would say "vitality." The purists say: "Give us one style throughout." "Give us life!" say the others.

Now the Renaissance was both pure and lively, but unfortu-nately it was not both at the same time. You have heard of the

STROZZI PALACE, FLORENCE
(*See p. 125*)

FIG. 88A. - FROM A MONUMENT IN FLORENCE

chairman who, being asked to return thanks after a lecture, said: "My friends, we have heard many things to-night that are both new and true; but unfortunately the things that are new are not true, and the things that are true are not new."

It might be said of the Renaissance that it was both pure and full of life; but — when it was pure, it was rather dull, and when it showed most vitality, it was "mixed." Every rule has its exceptions, and the exception to this one is Italy.

FIG. 88B. - FROM A VENETIAN PALACE

Here the Renaissance was brightest and purest and best at one and the same time: namely, at its birth. In France and Spain and England, it began by being "mixed," and became purer later on, and colder and duller; and the same might be said of Holland and Germany. In all these countries, the early or Transition stage was the cheerful one, when they had not quite made up their minds to accept this New Style, this Italian importation, and were content with grafting some Roman details onto a Gothic plan. Gradually they added more and more of these foreign details, and became more and more classic, and correct and pure, till they sickened of their purity and went in for licence — that is, the abuse of liberty. This period is known as the Rococo Style.

People seldom agree about the merits of any particular style, and we are prepared for a variety of opinions, but in the case of the Renaissance, the variety is rather overwhelming. One man calls it a weak and borrowed style, with no character of its own, non-constructive, its one idea concealment. Another describes it as an imposing, pleasing, dignified style, airy and magnificent. Could you believe that these different descriptions refer to the same style? Yet they are all true — in a sense. The Renaissance was all these things, but — at different times, and in different countries, and at different times in the same country: and the critics who express these contrary and contradictory opinions are often thinking of totally different things. One is thinking of Italian Renaissance; another of French Renaissance; another of English Renaissance; and yet another of German Renaissance. One is thinking of Italian Renaissance at its birth, when it was glowing and grand, another of French Renaissance in its later stage; a third of English Renaissance in its decline. No wonder they come to such different conclusions.

FIG. 88C. - FROM A PALACE IN FLORENCE

Still, there are certain features which we always associate with this style, and which are more or less characteristic of it as a whole. These are:—

The colossal columns, extending through several stories, which are common in later Renaissance, round-headed windows, heavy projecting cornices crowned with statuary, domes, balustrades (Fig. 88B and Plate XLI), broken (or interrupted) pediments and, above all, "rusticated masonry." This term is rather misleading, for there is nothing rustic about it. On the contrary, it is stiff and rigid: consisting of large

FIG. 88D. - FROM FERRARA

blocks of stone, with broad joints, from which the rough stonework projects boldly. The "rustication" is usually confined to the lower story, but sometimes there are bands of rustication carved at intervals across the walls and the columns or pilasters.

Among the many minor features characteristic of the Renaissance are:— scrolls, shields, garlands, festoons, and wreaths of fruit and flowers, cupids and angels, mirrors, masks and musical instruments, and gilding, and lions' heads — all, or nearly all, which you will see examples of in Figs. 88 if you look very carefully, and in the streets of your own city.

I hope the list is exhaustive enough to enable you to recognize a Renaissance building at a glance, whether you meet

FIG. 88E. - FROM THE BARGELLO, FLORENCE

it in England, or Scotland or Ireland, or France, or Germany, or in its own home — Italy.

THE ELIZABETHAN STYLE

It was a long time before the Renaissance got a firm footing in England. The English are a conservative race, not particularly hospitable to new ideas, and when this New Style made its appearance, they did not exactly open their arms to it. There was a long period of probation and trial, before they finally made up their minds to accept it. When at last they did so, it was a wholehearted surrender, complete and lasting, but the time had not come yet. Those early days of doubt, hesitation, and trial, of dilly-dally and shilly-shally, belong to the reign of Queen Elizabeth: hence, this Transition period is known as the Elizabethan Style.

The French also had a Transition Stage — the François Premier or Francis I period — and a delightful one it is. Plate XXXVIII is an example of the French Transition Period. It is almost entirely Gothic and Late Gothic (notice the flattened arch), but the pilasters at the side are ornamented with Renaissance detail. Like the French "Transition," our Elizabethan is a domestic architecture — an architecture of houses, not churches, and more especially of country-houses. There is a great charm about these picturesque Elizabethan mansions with their steep gables, bay windows, and fantastic chimneys. You know what a Bay Window is? One which juts out so as to form a bay or recess in the room. We generally call it a Bow Window, but that term seems more applicable to the semicircular window, which made its appearance later (Fig. 89). You will see many examples of the bay window in the colleges at Oxford and Cambridge, most of which belong to the Elizabethan style.

Another picturesque feature of this style is the Parapet which crowns the whole building. It is generally pierced into patterns — sometimes the piercing takes the form of a sentence, or the initial letters of the builder's name.

Talking of letters, the plan of the house was usually in the form of the letter H or E, with the entrance in the centre of the letter (Plate XXXIX). (The E may have been a compliment to Queen Elizabeth). Suppose we stand for a moment on the threshold and look in.

We see a grand entrance hall, with a huge fireplace, elaborately carved, and great logs crackling merrily, and sending up flames which cast dim shadows on the wall like Rembrandt pictures. All round, the oak-panelled walls are hung with tap-

FIG. 89. - ENGLISH RENAISSANCE. LILFORD HALL, NORTHANTS, 1635. (GOTCH)

estry and armour and portraits of ancestors. What an ideal background for a Christmas party! At one end of the hall is a gallery for the minstrels who used to sing and recite to the guests, while a handsome staircase leads up to another gallery or reception-room, and the guest chambers.

There are always two ways at least of describing a thing, and some people describe this Elizabethan style as "a charming commingling of the Classical and the Romantic, combining the best elements of both."

Others, not quite so complimentary, call it "a florid, incongruous style, exhibiting a hopeless confusion of ideas!"

Well, these critics are quite right. It was florid and it was incongruous, but it was also very picturesque and imposing and convenient. Another virtue it had: it was consistent with itself — consistently incongruous, if you like, but still consistent.

If the architecture was florid and mixed, so was the furniture, and so were all the interior decorations and details. Walter Scott describes some tapestry hangings in Kenilworth Castle, the subjects of which are decidedly "mixed" and incongruous — Abraham, and Alexander the Great, and Lady Fame, and the Prodigal Son, and Hunting and Hawking, together with forest scenes and pillars and arches, all mingled together in delightful confusion. "A mad world, my masters?" Yes, but there was a madder one coming — "a madder, merrier day!" and that day is known as the Rococo or Baroque Period.

ROCOCO

The Rococo is a debased style, marked by an excess of ornament, incongruous in subject, and bad in design (Plate XL). It pretends to be classical, but it is a very impure classical. The pillars are either too long or too short, dwarfs

THE TOMB OF CHRIST
(*See p. 132*)

PHOTO, *Haguard Du Nord*

ROCOCO PAVILION, ZWINGER PALANCE, DRESDEN
(SEE P. 134)

or giants. The capitals are neither Greek nor Roman, but a strange compound of their own. The corbels are reversed, the cornices are interrupted, and the pediments broken.

The sacred "Orders" were treated in the most cavalier fashion. All sorts of liberties were taken with them. The columns were made to do things they had never done before, such as standing broadside uppermost, or tapering downwards; and they were made to adorn objects they had never adorned before, such as chimney pots. Sometimes they were intersected by square blocks all the way up, till almost nothing was left of the column except its capital, and it was as much transformed and puzzled as to its identity as the old woman in the nursery tale — who cried — The friends of the dislocated one might well "bark and wail."

> "I have a little dog at home, and he knows me:
> If it be I, he will wag his little tail,
> But if it be *not* I, he will bark and he will wail."

Later on, things grew worse. It was not only the columns that lost their identity, but everything else, especially the gables. They broke out into curves (Fig. 89). And such curves, and such gables! They rose in perpendicular stories or stages, one above the other, each story a little narrower than the one below it, and with a curved volute or scroll at the side — a reversed volute, of course, and a double curve. For it was the age of Curves. They would have no more straight lines. They had had enough of them in the "Perpendicular"; now it was to be Curves for a change. And it was: Curves everywhere — curved cupids with curved bows and limbs, curved shells, and curved cornucopia (Fig. 88E), and curved shields and festoons and wreaths and garlands, and curved pediments (Fig. 88C), and curved consoles or brackets, and curved little curly-wurly things that look like "the ribbed sea sand," and are called rustications. It was a riot of curves. Every straight line was turned into a curved line, and every simple curve into a complex one—that is, a double curve; one that begins by going one way, and changes its mind in the middle and goes quite another way. The architecture was like the age in which it flourished. "Change for the sake of change," seemed to be its motto. An age of license and luxury, of periwigs and pigtails, of powder and patches. And the architecture reflected the age. The Germans call it the "Putz und Kopf" style; that is, the Periwig and Pigtail. It was a demoralized architecture, acknowledging no law, trampling on tradition, and breaking almost every principle of construction—a very carnival of architecture.

After a time, however, men tired of the license and extravagances of the Rococo, and there was a reaction in favor of sanity and symmetry.

THE ENGLISH RENAISSANCE
INIGO JONES AND CHRISTOPHER WREN

The Renaissance in England dates from the reign of the Stuarts: that is, the seventeenth century. Two names are inseparably associated with this period: Inigo Jones and Christopher Wren. We can scarcely think of the English Renaissance without thinking of these two men.

The style they introduced was the Grand Style, or the Italian Style, sometimes also called the Palladian Style. Everything is on the grand scale, imposing, dignified, classical: rich, yet restrained in detail. The most striking features are — the "Palladian Orders" — that is, the great colossal columns which extend through several stories of the façade; the "Pillar-

BANQUETING HALL, WHITEHALL, LONDON
(*SEE PP. 129, 140*)

and-Portico" entrances, which look like imposing miniature classical temples; and the handsome terraces with broad flights of steps leading to the formal, tree-clipped gardens.

This "Palladian Style" was named after Palladio, a famous Italian sculptor-architect who lived in the days of Michael Angelo, and just before the time of Inigo Jones. The latter admired Palladio so much that he went to Italy to study his works, and came back full of Palladio and his style, and modeled all his works on that style. They are said to be palatial, or palace-like, or Palladio-like: you will see many of them in London.

The finest of all is the Banqueting House, Whitehall (Plate XLI), which is part of a Royal Palace, and one of the grandest conceptions of the Renaissance style.

SIR CHRISTOPHER WREN

Inigo Jones was succeeded by Christopher Wren, the greatest of the Renaissance architects. He did not go to Italy like Jones, but studied in Paris, and with excellent results — for, among other famous buildings, he gave us St. Paul's, London (Plate XLII). Wren's opportunity came in the year 1666, when the City of London was almost destroyed by the Great Fire.

He was a rising young architect at the time, and he designed a grand plan for the rebuilding of the city. There was not money enough for all he wanted to do, but many of his designs were accepted, and he built about a score of parish churches, including Bow Church, Cheapside, with its original steeple; called after him the Wren Steeple. Among his other buildings are:

Kensington Palace, parts of Hampton Court Palace, Chelsea Hospital, and Greenwich Hospital (Fig. 90), and, best of all —

St. Paul's, London (Plate XLII)

which is not only Wren's masterpiece, but is considered by many to be the noblest structure in the Renaissance style in Great Britain. Its most striking feature is the DOME—and

FIG. 90. - ENGLISH - RENAISSANCE. GREENWICH HOSPITAL

whether you admire domes in general or not, I think you cannot help admiring this one, because it is one of the finest domes in Europe. It depends for its effect greatly upon the beautiful drum from which it springs. The drum is the upright part of a cupola or dome.

There is one part of St. Paul's which is a striking illustration of a Renaissance characteristic: namely, "concealment." It is the façade.

You will see that it has two stories with Corinthian col-

ST. PAUL'S LONDON

(See, p. 141.)

umns. Well, the upper story is a sham; the façade is merely a screen to add to the height and dignity of the cathedral — there is nothing behind it.

There are three things in St. Paul's that I need scarcely tell you to look out for — you could not well miss them: first, the Whispering Gallery high up in the cupola, where the slightest whisper is heard and re-echoed; secondly, the Golden Gallery above the dome, where you get a magnificent view of London; and thirdly, the ball on the very top of the cathedral, which you may perhaps be allowed to enter.

But beyond all that, there is the interest of the historic monuments, for many of our greatest men lie beneath the shadow of St. Paul's — Nelson, Wellington, Wolseley, and Christopher Wren himself. On his tomb is inscribed "Si monumentum quaeris, circumspice," which means, "If you wish to see his monument, look around."

ST. PETER'S, ROME

> "'The hand that rounded Peter's Dome,
> And groined the aisles of Christian Rome,
> Wrought in a sad sincerity:
> Himself from God he could not free;
> He builded better than he knew,
> The conscious stone to beauty grew.' —EMERSON.

The Cathedral of St. Paul's, London, is the noblest example of the Renaissance style in Great Britain; but not in the world. There is a nobler at Rome.

To see a style at its best we must see it in its own surroundings, with its own natural setting, its own local color. Emerson, the American writer, has a poem called "Each and All," in which he tells us how one morning he heard a little bird "singing at dawn on the alder bough," and was so enchanted with the song and the bird that he "brought him home in his nest at even, but," he adds sadly, "He sings the song, but it pleases not now,"

> "For I did not bring home the river and sky:
> He sang to my — "they sang to my eye!"

Yes! We want the river and sky — the yellow Tiber and the blue sky of Italy. We shall go to Rome and see St. Peter's (Plate XLIII).

Here it is! We cannot mistake that huge building, standing in the great piazza or square, with its semi-circular colonnade of light columns. How Roman-like that semi-circle is!

But what is this? Surely we have seen that great dome before? Yes! But not in its present position: not on the top of St. Peter's. It was a temple when last we saw it, and its name was the Pantheon.

How came it there?

You have heard of Michael Angelo, the famous sculptor and painter and architect — the most famous in all Italy. One day, looking at the Pantheon, he said: "I will raise the Pantheon into the sky! I will build a church and put the Pantheon on the top for a dome!"

And he did. And there it stands — the most magnificent creation of the Renaissance. It rises from a lofty "drum," and is surmounted by a "lantern," which stands out against the sky, leaving far below it the Colosseum and other monuments of the Eternal City.

Everything in St. Peter's is on a colossal scale. The columns are a hundred feet high. The figures below the dome, which look just life-size, are really giants. If they stood up, they would be twenty feet high.

ST. PETER'S, ROME

(SEE P. 144)

The very pen in the hand of St. Mark is nine feet long, though it looks like an ordinary quill.

No doubt the builders thought that by means of these colossal columns, which are all of one "Order" (the Corinthian), inside and outside, and by the gigantic details, they would obtain grandeur and simplicity at the same time. But they have the very opposite effect, for they dwarf the whole building. This is true of many other Renaissance churches. Few of them look as big as they are. The Gothic churches, on the contrary, look larger than they really are because the details are smaller and the whole space is divided into smaller parts, which adds to the apparent size.

There is only one point from which we can realize faintly the immense size of St. Peter's, and that is inside, at the foot of the altar, just under the dome, where we can see all four arms of the cross.

The interior of St. Peter's is characteristic of the Renaissance. It is all airy magnificence and gigantic splendor, full of marbles and mosaics, gilding, and gay colors — not just our idea of a church, but the Italians take their religion cheerfully.

St. Peter's is the most magnificent building in the world. It is higher than the Pyramids of Egypt. It is the Mecca of Italy, and is visited by thousands of pilgrims daily. Among others of less note, there once came to Rome a French woman of great genius, Madame de Staël, who wrote a story called Corinne, in which she describes St. Peter's, the Pantheon, and many other buildings in a fascinating way.

There also came to Rome a young girl named Anna Jameson, who loved pictures, statues, and beautiful buildings. Of course, she visited St. Peter's, not once but many times, and she tells in her diary how one morning she ascended the great dome, and even mounted into the gold ball, and got a bird's-eye view of the Eternal City. She had seen St. Peter's in every light — sunlight, moonlight, and twilight — and she thought she knew it in every aspect. But one evening, she saw it in a new light, so new and so wonderful that she felt as if she had never seen it before.

The new light was torchlight! Once a year, St. Peter's used to be illuminated from top to toe, or from foundation to summit, even to the gold Cross that crowns all. It was a very impressive sight, but one which we shall probably never see again because this interesting ceremony was performed for the last time in the year 1869, and it is not at all likely that it will be revived. Fortunately, we have Anna Jameson's description, which is a particularly vivid one. She says:

"We drove to the Piazza of St. Peter's to see the far-famed illumination of the church. The twilight closed rapidly round us. The long lines of statues along the roof and balustrades, faintly defined against the evening sky, looked like spirits come down to gaze. A great crowd of carriages and people on foot filled every avenue, but all was still, except when a half-suppressed murmur of impatience broke through the hushed silence of suspense. At length, on a signal, which was given by the firing of a cannon, the whole of the immense façade and dome, even up to the Cross on the summit, burst into a blaze, as if at the touch of an enchanter's wand. The carriages now began to drive rapidly round the piazza, each with a train of running footmen, flinging their torches round and dashing them against the ground. The shouts of the crowd, the stupendous building with all its architectural outlines and projections, defined in lines of living flame, the sparkling of the fountains, produced an impression far beyond anything I could have anticipated, and more like the gorgeous fictions of the Arabian Nights than any earthly reality."

THE SECOND CLASSICAL REVIVAL

THE REIGN OF SYMMETRY

There is not much more to tell. There were no new styles after the seventeenth century — just revivals — that is, a return to old styles.

This "Second Classical Revival" was a return to the Renaissance. It was a sort of second-hand Renaissance, but it had not the "go" in it of the first. It was tamer, quite as correct or more so, but cold. You remember how the extravagances of the Rococo period led to a reaction in favor of sanity and symmetry. Well, the symmetry had gone too far: it absorbed all else. This Second Classical Revival might be called — the Age of Symmetry.

Symmetry means equality, balance. It is opposed to proportion, where everything is unequal: one thing bigger or more important than the rest. There can be no proportion in equal things; they can have symmetry only. So if you like even numbers — twos, and fours, and sixes — you will like symmetry; but if you prefer odd numbers such as threes, and fives, and sevens, you will be on the side of proportion. The Greeks and Romans loved symmetry; the Gothic builders, proportion. I knew a little girl — a twin — who had a great feeling for symmetry. One day she was taken by her mother to visit a house where there was a new-born baby. After inspecting the mite with great interest, she began an earnest search round the room, pulling out drawers, and looking under the table and chairs, and below the bed, and behind the curtains.

"What are you looking for, darling?" asked her mother.

A little face looked up wistfully. "For the Other One! Mummy."

Some people are always looking for the "Other One," and will not be happy until they get it. They have a passion for symmetry. If you visit at their house, you will see everything in pairs. Twin pictures stare at you from opposite sides of the wall. Twin shepherds and shepherdesses with arms interlaced, flanked by twin vases and twin matchboxes, adorn the mantelpiece. These people are victims of symmetry. They would refuse a portrait of their grandfather if they did not have one of their grandmother on the other side to balance it. They remind one of the French monarch of whom Madame de Maintenon said — "He prefers to endure all the draughts of the doors in order that they may be opposite one another — you must perish in symmetry!"

Now that is typical of this "Second Classical Revival." "You must perish in symmetry!" And it is a dead symmetry, for the spirit that should have animated it — that did animate the First Classical Revival — was dying out, or had died out, and only the form remained. If you compare it with the First Classical Revival, or Renaissance, you will find a great difference. The latter got its inspiration from the Greek and Roman masterpieces, the actual buildings, and the writings of Vitruvius, and other men of genius who describe them. This Second Classical Revival got its inspiration from the Renaissance itself. It is therefore a copy of a copy, an imitation of imitators. Its models are not the Parthenon and the Pantheon, but the Renaissance copies of these. Its exponents were not inspired by Pheidias and Vitruvius, but by their admirers and imitators — Michael Angelo and Palladio, Inigo Jones and Christopher Wren. Its architects were not men of original genius, but men of exact knowledge.

Such a second or third-hand inspiration does not count for much. It is apt to be regarded with feelings of cold esteem rather than enthusiasm, and you will not be surprised to hear that after a time our forefathers tired of this "architecture of footrule," and went in search of something new.

The result was a succession of revivals, more or less literal — that is, an exact copy — more or less successful. All the styles you have read about in this book were tried in turn. Sometimes several styles would be running at once. For a long time, the Gothic and the Greek were very popular. They seemed to be running a race, and it was difficult to say which would win. Sometimes the one would seem to be getting ahead, sometimes the other: and the friends and partisans of each were very excited, and loud in the praises of their own particular style. This "Battle of the Styles" is interesting reading, but we cannot go into it here. There is only space for a few words about the Grecian Revival, which will perhaps interest you most, because you have heard so much about the bringing to England of the Elgin Marbles, which helped to bring about this revival by creating an interest in Greece. You must often have seen examples of this new Greek style — buildings more or less like the Parthenon — and you may have wondered what they were doing so far from their native land.

For instance, there is the British Museum, in London, and the Church of St. Pancras, whose porch is an exact copy of the porch of the Erechtheum at Athens, the one with the caryatides; and there is St. George's Hall, Liverpool; and the Royal High School, and National Gallery, Edinburgh (Plate XLIV); besides many other beautiful examples in America.

SCOTTISH NATIONAL GALLERY
(*See* p. 150)

And very admirable most of these buildings are, with excellent proportions, and quiet and refined details. We feel that we ought to admire them immensely, and be deeply moved at sight of them, and we are surprised and disappointed with ourselves at our own lack of enthusiasm, our lukewarm admiration. But the truth is that a Greek temple looks best in its own country. It will never be the same anywhere else: it will be Greek only in name. The spirit is wanting — and the sunshine, and the sculpture. A Grecian temple under southern skies is one thing, and a Grecian temple in a London fog, or an Edinburgh east wind whistling through its grey columns, is quite another thing. And then there is the statuary. The Grecian temple was a framework for the Grecian sculpture. Every frieze and wall, and pediment of it was taken advantage of for the purpose of exhibiting that sculpture, without which it is a mere shell, perfect in form, but without expression; beautiful, but lifeless —

> "So coldly sweet, so deadly fair,
> We start! for soul is wanting there!"

GOOD-BYE!

Well, we have traveled far in search of The Beautiful, and seen and sampled many buildings, from a house as simple as "The House that Jack built" to all the gilded glories of a Renaissance palace. And now that we are at the end of our journey, I wonder, supposing some good fairy offered us our choice, which of them all would we choose?

It would be rather a difficult matter, would it not? At least, I hope so. I should like to think that we can enjoy many different styles, and would bear up manfully if we suddenly fell heir to a Tudor mansion or a Renaissance palace when we had set our heart on a Norman castle. A young friend of mine, who was not tried in this way, but thought it best to prepare for all emergencies, considered the question carefully, and this was her conclusion: "I would like best of all," she says, "an old ruin, with moss and ivy and creepers growing all over it; but if I had to build a house, I would not be able to build a ruin, so I think I would like next best an elaborate spick-and-span new building, with statues of men and women all round."

Well, I think we will agree with the first part at any rate. We all love a ruin. There is something fascinating about it. What a pity that we cannot live in a ruin! Nor worship in one! Though we may picnic. Have you ever wondered why a ruin should be so fascinating? What is the secret of its charm? Is it only because of its picturesque-ness, its ruggedness, or raggedness?

I think the explanation lies deeper than that. There are many people who care nothing for the picturesque, and who yet are strangely attracted by a ruin. They are touched by its pathos. That is the secret of its appeal. It has a story to tell. It speaks to them of the Past; of the men and women who lived there, of the children who played there, the friends who gathered under its roof, the sounds of merry laughter that echoed in its halls, the stories of love and adventure that its walls could tell — of all that Past Life which we associate with it and which is its soul. All that is in the ruin, and all that we think of when we look at it. That is the secret of its charm. It speaks to our imagination and to our heart.

And something of the same charm we want in our architecture, something that will speak to our imagination and to our heart, that will speak to us of things we want to know, and show us things we want to see, and remind us of things we want to remember. An architecture that will call up Nature's Cathedrals, her giant columns, her stained windows, her fretted vaults, her turrets, her spires and pinnacles, an architecture whose inspiration has been caught from Nature's own woods and plains: that has in it the strength of the hills and the haunting beauty of the forest; the mystery of the silent stars, and of those other lesser stars "that in earth's firmament do shine."

Such an architecture would be worth praying for, and — paying for; and if you know one that does any or all these things I wonder if you can tell me its name.

Does it begin with a G?